The Fire Within

Pierre Drieu La Rochelle

THE FIRE
WITHIN

<small>Translated from the French by Richard Howard</small>

New York : Alfred·A·Knopf : 1965

L. C. catalog card number: 65–10062

THIS IS A BORZOI BOOK,
PUBLISHED BY ALFRED A. KNOPF, INC.

FIRST AMERICAN EDITION

Originally published in French as *Le Feu Follet*.
© 1931, 1963 by Éditions Gallimard.

The Fire Within

1   At that moment, Alain looked intently at Lydia. But he had been looking at her the same way ever since she arrived in Paris, three days ago. What did he expect? A sudden illumination about her or about himself.

Lydia was looking at him too, her eyes dilated but not intense. And soon she turned her head away, dropped her eyelids, absorbed. In what? In herself? Was that what she was really like, full of a murmurous, placated rage that swelled her neck and her belly? It was only the mood of a moment. It was past already.

And so he stopped staring at her. Once again, sensation had slid away, elusive as a viper between two stones. He lay still for a moment, on top of her, but tense, unyielding, propped on his elbows. Then, as his flesh forgot itself, there was nothing to do but roll over beside her. She was stretched out near the edge of the bed; he had just enough room to lie on his side, close against her, farther up on the mattress.

Lydia opened her eyes again. All she saw was a hairy chest, no head. It didn't matter: she had felt nothing very violent either, yet the switch had been tripped, and that was the only sensation she had ever known, not permeating but precise.

The weak light shivering in the ceiling bulb barely suggested, through the scarf Alain had wrapped around it, unknown walls and furniture.

"Poor Alain, how uncomfortable you look," she said after a pause, and moved over, taking her time. "Cigarette," she asked.

"It's been a long time . . ." he murmured expressionlessly.

He reached for the pack he had remembered to put on the night-table when they went to bed several minutes before. It was unopened, but the third that day. He slit it with a fingernail, and they took pleasure, as if they had long been deprived of it, in extracting from the tight cluster two small white cylinders, crammed with fragrant tobacco.

Without bothering to turn her head as she rolled onto her back, twisting her lovely shoulder, she groped blindly on the other night-table for her purse, out of which she took a lighter. The two cigarettes flared. The ceremony was over, they would have to talk.

But talking didn't bother them the way it used to; each one, no longer afraid to reveal himself, had reached the point of finding the other's reality already brief, but still enjoyable: they had slept together about twelve times.

"It's nice, Alain, seeing you again for a while, alone."

"I've made a mess of your trip."

He was not attempting to apologize for what had happened. And she made no complaint; from the moment she had come to him, she ran the risk of such incidents. Still, wasn't she making a tiny secret effort to convince herself that out of three days in Paris, with Alain, she had to spend one at the police station, after being picked up with him in a narcotics raid?

"And you're leaving this morning," he added in a voice thickened with resentment.

She was sailing on the *Leviathan*, on which she had arrived. But to do so, she had had to spend all the previous evening on the telephone, for she had not booked return passage from New York, even though she had expected to be in Paris only a few days. Had that been carelessness, or a secret intention of staying? In which case, it must have been the police incident that had convinced her to go back—the night spent on a chair surrounded by smelly detectives who blew smoke in her face, while Alain sank into a defeated stupor that had surprised her. Despite her being an American and the prompt intervention of friends, the humiliation had lasted several hours.

Still, she had persisted.

"Alain, we've got to get married."

She was telling him that, because it was to say such a thing that she had taken the *Leviathan* in the first place.

Six months before, a young divorcée, she had become engaged to Alain one evening, in a bathroom in New York City. But three days later she had married someone else, a stranger, whom she had left soon afterward.

"My divorce is coming through soon."

"I can't say the same for mine," Alain answered, but his nonchalance was overdone.

"I know you still love Dorothy."

That was true, but it didn't keep him from wanting to marry Lydia.

"But Dorothy isn't the kind of woman you need, she hasn't got enough money and she lets you run around. You need a wife who won't leave you for a minute; otherwise you get too sad, ready to do anything."

"You know me pretty well," Alain jeered. His eyes had gleamed for a moment.

He was still amazed that a woman really wanted to marry him. For years he had dreamed of getting his hands on a woman; it meant money, protection, no more problems. There had been Dorothy, but she wasn't rich enough, and he hadn't known how to hold on to her. Would he be able to keep this one? Did he even have her now?

"I've never stopped wanting to marry you," she continued, neither apology nor irony in her voice.

"But I had this involvement that got in my way."

For years she had been living in a world where it was understood that nothing had to be explained or justified, where everything was done by whim.

The same rules kept Alain from smiling.

"You have to come to New York and face Dorothy, even if you go back to her. We'll get married there. When can you leave? When will you be cured?"

She always spoke in the same even tone, without showing any eagerness. And she made no attempt to interpret Alain's expression; she lay on her back smoking, while Alain, leaning on one elbow, stared past her.

"I am already."

"Still, if the police hadn't come, you'd have started smoking."

"No I wouldn't. Maybe you'd have started; I would have watched you."

"You would? Anyway, you went to the men's room in the restaurant to take some heroin."

"No, going to the men's room is an old habit of mine."

It was true that Alain had not taken any heroin, but

going to the toilet had always been an alibi to justify
his frequent absences.

"Besides, Alain, they say there is no such thing as a
cure."

"You know I don't want to kill myself on the stuff."

It was a terribly vague answer: but Lydia never
asked questions and never expected answers.

"When we're married, we'll take a trip to Asia," she
suggested.

She believed that action was the way to settle
everything.

"That's right, Asia or China."

She smiled. She sat on the edge of the bed.

"Oh! Alain dear, it's broad daylight, I've got to get
back to the hotel."

An unnameable element was flowing through the
curtains.

"Your train isn't until ten."

"I know. But I have so much to do. And there's a
woman I have to see."

"Where?"

"At the hotel."

"She'll be asleep."

"I'll wake her."

"She won't like that."

"I don't care."

"All right."

But as he was about to get up, he had a premonition, a pang.

"Lie down again, come back."

"No, dear, it was fine, I'm quite content. Just kiss me."

He gave her a kiss serious enough to make her want to stay in Paris.

"I love you in a very special way," she said slowly, looking at last into Alain's handsome, eroded face.

"Thank you for coming." He said this with that subdued emotion he sometimes betrayed, whose unexpected appearance would suddenly attach people to him. But, as usual, he yielded to an absurd impulse of modesty or elegance and jumped up from the bed. Then she did the same, and disappeared into the bathroom.

While she was removing from her womb the seal of her sterility and then performing a brief ablution, the mirror reflected, without her showing any interest, beautiful legs and shoulders, a face that was exquisite but seemed anonymous in its pallor, and stupid because of an affected coldness. Her skin was the leather of a de luxe piece of luggage that had traveled a great deal, strong and defiled. Her breasts were forgotten emblems. She dried herself, spreading her thighs where the muscles had begun to go slack. Then she came back into the bedroom to get her purse.

Alain was walking up and down, smoking another cigarette. She took one too. Alain looked at her, without really seeing her; indulging an old habit, his gaze explored the room for some laughable, doubtless agonizing detail. But this hired cell, through which an uninterrupted procession of livestock passed, was more banal than a public urinal; there weren't even any graffiti. Only stains, on the walls, on the rug, on the furniture. One imagined other stains on the sheets, hidden by the chemistry of laundering.

"What are you looking for?"

"Nothing."

This body of Alain's, one hand holding a cigarette, was a phantom, even emptier than Lydia's. His belly was flat, yet the sick fat of his face made him look bloated. He had muscles, but the idea of his lifting a weight would have seemed incredible. A handsome mask, but one made of wax. His thick hair might have been a wig.

Lydia had returned to the bathroom to paint a strange caricature of life on her dead woman's face. White on white, then red, then black. Her hand was trembling. She stared without pity or alarm at the subtle stigmata of spiderwebs at the corners of her mouth and eyes.

"I like these dirty hotels," she called to Alain, "they're the only places in the world that seem intimate to me, because I've never gone to one except with you."

"Yes," he sighed.

She pleased him, because she said only necessary things. He sensed, moreover, that this necessity was slight.

She was back in the bedroom, rummaging through her purse for a checkbook, then a pen, all the while staring at Alain. There was a keen satisfaction in her look, but no hope. She set one foot on the bed and wrote on her knee. Such nakedness, brutally stripped of coquetry, could not be arousing.

She held out a check to him. He took it and looked at it.

"Thank you."

He had been counting on this money, and last night he had spent all that remained of the two thousand francs she had given him on her arrival in Paris. Now she had written: 10,000. But he owed the sanitarium 5,000 and 2,000 to a friend who had supplied him with drugs. Once it would have seemed a miracle to be given ten thousand francs all at once, but now it was a wasted gesture. Lydia was richer than Dorothy, but not rich enough. Alain's exacerbated poverty was an ever-widening abyss which only an enormous fortune could fill—the kind that doesn't turn up every day.

He smiled at her sweetly.

"I'll get dressed, Alain dear."

He picked up his scattered clothing and went in his turn to the bathroom.

A little later, they walked downstairs. The corridors were empty; they sensed, behind the doors, a heavy, universal sleep. A wan and disheveled chambermaid wrenched herself out of an armchair where she was curled up snoring, and opened the door for them. Since Alain had given all the money he had to the taxi-driver who had brought them here, he slipped off his wristwatch and handed it to her. The girl was startled out of her stupor; yet she threw him a resentful look, for she had no lover to whom she could pass on the gift.

It was November, but not very cold. Day slid over the night like a wet rag over a dirty pane of glass. They went down the rue Blanche, between garbage cans piled high with offerings. Lydia walked ahead, tall, shoulders back, on heels of clay. In the gray dawn, her makeup glowed, one feverish patch here, one there.

They came to the Place de la Trinité. The café on the corner of the rue Saint-Lazare was open; they went in. The working people gathering their strength inside stared for a moment of knowing pity at this wreck of a handsome couple. They drank two or three cups of coffee, then left.

"Alain, let's walk a little more."

He nodded. But the Chaussée-d'Antin depressed him, and he suddenly hailed a solitary taxi which was rolling along like a ball on a ghostly billiard table. She frowned, but he looked so sad that she checked her protest.

"I can't take you to the train," he declared hoarsely, slamming the cab door. "If I'm not back at the sanitarium by eight, the doctor will throw me out."

He was genuinely sorry. She believed it, for no man was so attentive as Alain to all the little ceremonies of feeling.

"All right, Alain, come to New York as soon as you can. I'll send you money; I'm sorry I don't have more today. I'm sure what I gave you won't be enough. And we'll get married. Kiss me."

She offered him a mouth that curved cleanly, though it tasted of the night's bitterness. He kissed her valiantly. What a beautiful face despite the makeup, the fatigue, and a certain ritual pride. She could have loved him, but he had probably scared her off, for good this time.

Suddenly he realized he was going to be alone again, and flinging himself back against the seat, he let out a violent moan.

"Alain, what is it!"

She grabbed his hand, as if she had taken hope. Their resigned indifference, their calm affectation cracked.

"Come to New York. I have to go back."

Alain did not want to shout: Why do you have to? Yet he knew she had no real reason. Lydia, for her part, felt much too weak to save Alain from what he had always been told was his fate.

They reached the hotel. He jumped out, rang the bell, and kissed her hand. She stared at him again, her huge watery blue eyes wide apart above her cheeks. That poor, charming boy—leaving him meant handing him over to his worst enemy, himself, abandoning him to this gray dawn in the rue Cambon, with the mournful trees of the Tuileries at one end. But she took refuge in the decision she had made as a precaution: to stay only three days in Paris. Alain tightened his lips, pulled himself together, and hoped she would stay in the narrow category of pretty woman she belonged to, unaware of the very fact that she was in love. Then this dawn would stay gray, there would never be any sun.

"Take me out to Saint-Germain," he murmured in an exhausted voice to the driver, while the heavy hotel door closed behind an ankle as fine as the silk that covered it.

The taxi drove him, somnolent and chilled, toward the sanitarium of Doctor de la Barbinais.

2 ALAIN DID NOT COME DOWN FROM HIS
room until lunchtime.

The dining-room, the lounge, the corridors, the
stairways were lined with literature: Doctor de la
Barbinais had not hesitated to expose the neurasthen-
ics in his care to portraits of all the writers who for
two centuries had won renown by their sufferings.
With a collector's innocent perversity, he arranged his
gallery so that the substantial faces of the nineteenth
century's dreamers gradually yielded to the thread-
bare ones of certain contemporaries. But, for him as
for his guests, only celebrity was involved. For Alain,
the place could have meant something else; but he
saw himself, here, in one of those museums he never
visited, and so passed quickly by.

Everyone was already at table, around Doctor de la Barbinais and his wife. These communal meals seemed to Alain the most incredible moments of his stay in a place that combined the equally horrible characteristics of a sanitarium and a boarding-house.

He was forced to look at the faces that surrounded the table. These were not lunatics, only light-headed: the doctor made sure his clientele was manageable.

Mademoiselle Farnoux smiled at Alain with meager lust. Farnoux, the Farnoux Foundries, cannons and shells. She was a little girl between forty and sixty, bald, with a black wig on her bloodless skull. Her parents had been old when she was born; sickly, insubstantial, she lived among her millions in incurable want. From time to time, she came to Doctor de la Barbinais for a "cure" from the ever more exquisite fatigue caused not by life but by watching others live. A childhood in cotton wool had taught her early to save her breath; even so, her strength exhausted, she had to stop every three months and temporarily entomb herself. During the moments when she pretended to be alive, she was, it is true, feverishly active. Escorted by an enormous chauffeur who carried her from salon to salon, and a long-suffering old secretary who gave her her enemas and pasted stamps on her letters, she ran from one end of Europe to the other, nibbling celebrities. She was famished for vitality; the little she had was concentrated in a single effort—to discover more in others. Although her temperament tended toward the finical, she despised whatever resembled it, and thrust herself upon the most explosive natures. Before a Russian writer with the fists of a stevedore, she smothered a tiny cry, deeply offended, yet she clung to that blood-steeped mass of flesh.

A remote but strident craving still lured her along other paths than those of glory. She carried a seed of lechery which had never been able to sprout and which stirred in her brain like a dead spore. She could not find satisfaction in the spectacle afforded by her chauffeur, a pederast who wriggled his heavy shoulders whenever a young man appeared, nor in the mild and, moreover, purely allusive contacts of her wretched companion; she was compelled to circle with submissive smiles and ignominious leers around any creature who had some talents for seduction and was willing to market them.

She suffered from her eternal regret whenever she was with Alain, whose bitter successes she had long ago tracked down in those dubious drawing-rooms where she rubbed elbows with the fakes and tramps of every vice.

Alain's other neighbor, the Marquis d'Averseau, seemed to epitomize everything Mademoiselle Farnoux coveted: a great name, since he was a descendant of the Maréchal d'Averseau; literary status, since he had written a *History of the Sodomite French Princes;* and, finally, a place in the chronicle of minor scandals. But he was hideous; only genius could have compensated for the green teeth beneath his swollen and suppurating lips. And his provincial anecdotes were definitely second-hand.

Beyond M. d'Averseau sat Mademoiselle Cournot, who, no less than Mademoiselle Farnoux, ogled Alain. She was enormous and skeletal. Despite the efforts of her father Baron Cournot, the author of several books on the philosophy of hygiene, solid flesh had never grown on her superseded bones, and Bichette Cournot stalked through her times like a poor plesiosaur escaped from a museum. She was passionate, but men fled her immoderate embraces. Whence a raging neurasthenia. Since no one paid any attention to her, she always assumed she was alone; at the Barbinais' table, she would every now and then, through the silk of her dress, scratch her long, snakeskin breasts.

Further down, two men were talking: M. Moraire and M. Brême. Both had been financiers and had considerably increased the fortunes they had inherited. But domestic troubles had finished off their degenerate nerves: cuckolded, tormented by perverse children, the Catholic banker and the Jewish broker had crossed paths, at Doctor de la Barbinais's sanitarium, which had long run parallel. They nursed a ceremonious hatred toward one another, with all the intensity of mutual consideration Jews and Christians can show.

Finally, Madame de la Barbinais. She was the only madwoman in the house. Though she incessantly obliged her husband to make love to her, her enormous womb still cried famine. Several times she had entered Alain's room, her cheeks purple, both hands clutching at the panic of all her organs, for the itch working in her uterus seemed to spread to her liver, her stomach. She gagged obscenely. Alain talked to her so good-naturedly that his words affected her like a sedative; lurching, she left his room and hurled herself on the doctor once more.

The doctor was a nervous jailer. His huge round eyes swiveled above cheeks scored by the terror of losing his boarders, and the little beard that substituted for a chin trembled incessantly.

All these people were eating and gossiping. Alain, mute, gazed at the carafe of red wine in front of him. He wasn't drinking at all: the day he had left another sanitarium, after a previous cure, he had walked into the first bar he came to and, suddenly craving something that would burn his throat, had gulped down a liter of the strongest wine he could buy. The alcohol, after his long abstinence, had had the effect of a jet of ether. In the street, he had begun to shout and insult passers-by. He had been taken to the police station.

"You were in Paris last night," sighed Mademoiselle Farnoux gluttonously.

Everyone in the house knew Alain had spent the night out, everyone was envious, but also, and especially, everyone was terrified. And their terror reached the proportions of scandal; all these valetudinarians censured Alain who was playing with the gods of their panic, with disease and with death.

"Some lovely person must have been very happy to have you back," Mademoiselle Farnoux continued.

"Some lovely persons aren't hard to please."

"But you are."

"Don't you believe it."

"If you weren't, you wouldn't be where you are."

As she pronounced these words which seemed brimming with understanding and sympathy, her blue eyes hardened. If Alain had opened his arms to her, with the one proviso that she share the risks and excesses people had whispered about, she would have refused, for she clung like a miser to the sickly treasure of her life; still, she begrudged him his temerity and almost rejoiced to see him paying for it, for Alain was pale and his features drawn.

"You've never been to America?" Alain asked mechanically.

"No, I've barely had time to get to know our old Europe. And the brutality over there would kill me.

But you've been there, haven't you? I hear you were a great success."

She thought how those American women must have given Alain money without counting it; she would have counted.

M. d'Averseau took advantage of this moment's thought to start a conversation; but his sour disposition led him as usual onto dangerous ground.

"Have you read *L'Action Française* this morning? The Maurras thing is absurd, of course, but there's an article on the court of Louis XIV that really goes too far. Some wretched provincial schoolteacher holding Racine's world over Proust's. But just read the Princess Palatine's letters: people had the same tastes then that they do today."

"I never read *L'Action Française*," snapped Mademoiselle Farnoux, who had preserved from her family's plebeian origin a certain hatred of reactionary opinions.

"I have to read it because my whole family does," M. d'Averseau continued plausibly, "but I don't like it. I was saying to my uncle just the other evening . . ."

He was telling the truth; his vice or his weak apprehension made even the slightest show of violence repugnant to him.

Moreover, he scorned Maurras's common birth and considered untimely the zeal of so many *petits bourgeois* for values whose tinkling debris supplied his own adornment.

"How is the Duke?" asked Mademoiselle Farnoux, who became amiable again at the thought of all the glittering titles accumulated by the d'Averseau family.

"Better, for the time being," answered M. d'Averseau, pleased to regain his ascendancy over the Foundries. . . . "That young man's brought back a nasty look from Paris; he was handsome a few years ago."

"He's still handsome enough to keep you looking at him."

"That no longer matters to anyone but you."

Alain did not feel the eyes of these people upon him; in recent months he had grown insensitive to the ubiquitous petty gossip around him.

Resolutely avoiding Mademoiselle Farnoux's politi-

cal conversation, he pretended to chat with Madame
de la Barbinais.

He met with the same sighs.

"Another night on the town," she murmured in a
choked voice.

"It was a very well-behaved night."

"Well, you don't look too bad. You must go back to
bed this afternoon, and sleep some more. Yes, go back
to bed, back to bed."

"Why is it, M. Brême, that you always monopolize
M. Moraire?" the doctor called across the table, con-
cerned to extend the conversation to all the guests.
"We'd all like to follow your discussion."

M. Brême and M. Moraire were both given to mys-
ticism. The latter's confessor had recommended several handbooks of watered-down Thomism, and M.
Moraire did his best to defend himself against the attacks of M. Brême, who was much better versed in
Christian theology, and may have been considering
conversion at the same time that he tormented his
neighbor.

Mademoiselle Cournot peered at the two men and

exclaimed with unexpected violence: "Oh, yes! That would be so interesting!"

But her eyes remained blank.

M. Brême and M. Moraire nodded importantly.

The wagging heads made Alain burst out laughing: Bichette looked at him with wild eyes.

Fortunately, luncheon was soon over. Alain avoided coffee in the drawing-room and went upstairs to his room.

It was raining outside, and he watched in terror as the rusty, dripping branches beat against his window. Alain was afraid of the country, and November on this humid estate, surrounded by gloomy suburbs, could only increase his fear.

Yet he liked his room, which, despite the dim light, was more prepossessing than all the hotel rooms he had inhabited after leaving his family. He lit a cigarette and looked around him.

The things on the table and the mantel were meticulously arranged. In the ever-narrowing circle in which he lived, everything counted. On the table there were letters and bills, divided into two piles. Then a stack of cigarette packages, and a pile of matchboxes. A pen. A large briefcase with a lock. On the night-table, detective stories or pornography, American magazines and avant-garde reviews. On the mantel, two objects: one a delicate piece of machinery, a perfectly flat platinum chronometer, the other a hideously vulgar painted plaster statuette of a naked woman that he had bought at a fair and took with him everywhere. He insisted it was pretty, but he was pleased that it polluted his life.

Photographs and newspaper clippings were stuck in the mirror's frame. A beautiful woman, taken full face, leaned back and displayed the lovely tendons stretched tight between chin and neck, a mouth with elusive edges, the twin holes of the nostrils, the uneven horizon of the eyebrows. A man, also leaning backward but photographed from behind, presented an expanse of forehead bounded at the far edge by a tufted rim, above which rose the foreshortened promontory of a nose. Between these two photographs, a news item pasted on the glass with four stamps reduced the human mind to two dimensions and left it no way out.

This room, too, had no way out; it was his private

eternity. For years he had had no home, and yet he
had his place in this ideal prison which remade itself
for him every evening, wherever he was. His cham-
bered anxiety was here, like a little box inside a larger
one. A mirror, a window, a door. The door and the
window opened onto nothing. The mirror opened only
onto himself.

Surrounded, isolated, Alain, in the last stage of his
withdrawal, paused over a few objects. In the absence
of people, who disappeared as soon as he left them,
and often even sooner, these objects gave him the illusion that he was still able to touch something outside
himself. And thus Alain had fallen into a shabby
idolatry; increasingly, he came to depend on the preposterous objects his abrupt, sardonic whims elected.
For the savage (and the child), objects palpitate; a
tree, a rock are more suggestive than a lover's body,
and he calls them gods because they trouble his blood.
But for Alain's imagination, the objects were not
points of departure; it was to them that his mind returned exhausted after a brief, futile journey through
the world. Out of dryness of heart, out of irony, he
had forbidden himself to entertain ideas about the

world. Philosophy, art, politics, morality—any system seemed to him an impossible rodomontade. Hence, unreinforced by ideas, the world was so insubstantial that it offered him no support. Only solids kept their shape.

In which he was deceived. He did not realize that what still gave them a semblance of form in his eyes was the residue of ideas which he had received in spite of himself from his education and out of which he unconsciously modeled these bits of matter. He would have laughed if anyone had asserted a secret connection, unacknowledged or denied by him, between the idea of justice, for example, and the obsession with symmetry that kept his room so orderly. He prided himself on being ignorant of the idea of truth, but rejoiced over a pile of matchboxes. For the savage, an object is the food which makes his mouth water; for the decadent, it is an excrement to which he vows a coprophagic worship.

Today, Alain gazed more imploringly than ever at all the things that surrounded him: Lydia's departure had touched him, doubling and deepening Dorothy's absence. He felt increasingly hemmed in by the circumstances he had allowed to accumulate around him. And what more terrifying sign than this: a captious logic had imprisoned him in an orbit from which he had tried to escape by every kind of outburst. That quartet of quiet crackpots drinking coffee down in the drawing-room, beneath the portraits of Constant and Baudelaire, was his family all over again: his mother, steeped in a timid nostalgia for love; his father who reproached himself for having reached old age with no more to show than the savings of a second-rate engineer; his divorced sister who didn't work; each one daydreaming in front of the other two. Years of insufficient efforts, which had not multiplied each other, let him fall back to zero.

He stood there, the cigarette scorching his lips, without a single resource, either inside or outside himself.

Then the usual reaction occurred. On the bare walls that confined his soul, he suddenly saw, of the few fetishes that adorned them, only the one which epitomized all the rest: money. He took Lydia's check out of his wallet, sat down at his table, and laid it flat in front of him. He became totally absorbed in the contemplation of this rectangle of paper charged with power.

Alain, since his first experiences of desire as an adolescent, had thought only of money. He was separated from it by the almost insuperable barrier of his laziness, his secret and virtually immutable determination never to seek it by working. But this fatal distance was the very thing that had awakened his interest. He always had money, yet never had any. Always a little, never a lot. It was a fluid and furtive glamour that perpetually ran between his fingers, but never thickened to any consistency. Where did it come from? Everyone had given it to him: friends, women. Having tried ten different jobs, he had even earned it, but in absurd amounts. He would often have two or three thousand francs in his pocket, without ever being sure of having as much the next day.

Today, he had ten thousand francs in front of him. He had never wangled ten thousand francs from anyone, all at once. Except from Dorothy at Monte Carlo, and that was to gamble with. He didn't like gambling:

gambling for him was only an excuse to ask Dorothy for money. But he gambled with it all the same, and lost it.

Ten thousand francs, then, was more than his usual loot, but it wasn't enough. It was nothing. He owed two hundred thousand francs to begin with; and then his ability to spend a thousand francs in an evening had increased year by year.

Of course, he had always doubted the meaning of the future, but the stark reality of that doubt had seized him only lately. He was discovering that there was a limit to borrowing, that it was impossible to make a habit of what his few solvent friends regarded as an exception. He was tired of that perpetual, spasmodic, and feeble extortion, whose limit he knew was never more than two or three thousand francs. He sensed that the main source of his credit, his youth, was exhausted.

The question was, would Lydia give him another ten thousand, twenty thousand, thirty thousand francs?

If she did, he would have to go to New York. If he

went to New York, he would have to stop taking drugs.

Yet this very evening he would start taking drugs again, because he had ten thousand francs.

Money, epitomizing the universe for him, was in its turn epitomized by drugs. Money, outside the meticulous garment of his hotel room, was the night.

That was the meaning of Lydia's check, lying on the table. It was night, it was drugs. It was certainly no longer Lydia, whom night, whom drugs, erased. Intoxication in the night. And night and intoxication, in the long run, were only sleep. That was all he was: night and sleep. Why try to struggle against his destiny? Why had he tormented himself all these months, made himself suffer? He had been frightened; at a certain moment he had discovered that chain of cause and effect which, coming full circle, annihilated him: drugs made him lose his women and his friends. And without either, no more money, therefore no more drugs.

Unless this was the ultimate dose on which you finish up and disappear. Well, it was time: these ten thousand francs, a few more nights, the last ones. Around six this evening he would go back to Paris and plunge deep into the definitive night.

Meanwhile, he had stretched out on his bed, and since he had not slept long enough that morning, he dozed off.

3   AT FOUR O'CLOCK, ALAIN WAS AWAKENED
by someone knocking at his door. It was Doctor de la
Barbinais.

"I've disturbed you, my friend. I'm sorry: you
needed the rest."

"Sit down, Doctor."

Alain remained stretched out on his bed. The return
to life, after that heavy sleep, scored his face with a
desolation that made the doctor's beard tremble.

"You spent the night out; it doesn't matter, provided
you didn't do anything silly."

"No, I didn't take any, I was with someone . . ."

"Oh, good."

The doctor seemed delighted. He was counting on
women to distract Alain from drugs.

But for that, Alain needed to like women a great deal, and at least one of the women he knew needed to have a positive response to virility.

Alain frowned in a way that made Doctor de la Barbinais's smile disappear.

"I'm going to start again."

"No, listen . . ."

"What else do you expect me to do?"

"No letter from America yet?"

"There won't be one."

"Of course there will. Be patient."

"I'm not the patient type, even though I've done nothing but wait all my life."

"Wait for what?"

"I don't know."

"But today, right now, you know very well what you're waiting for. You know you love your wife, and you know she loves you. When she finds out you're making an effort to change your way of life, she'll surely help you."

Alain, at the doctor's instigation, had written Dorothy a letter assuring her of his recovery and asking her to come back to him. He counted in turn on Lydia and on Dorothy, and was sure of neither.

"She left me because she realized I could never give up drugs."

"But you're giving them up right now."

"You know perfectly well I'm not."

"I consider you to be completely cured."

"It won't last. Starting tonight . . ."

"At least wait for your wife's answer."

"I tell you she won't answer."

He was despising himself for having taken the old man into his confidence. This silly pontiff, Alain thought, carried hypocrisy to the point of being genuinely kind, the better to catch his clients in the trap of morality.

It was actually fear, not kindness, that incited the doctor to reason with Alain. He carefully avoided treating real melancholia, and confined himself to calm and opulent fits of depression; he had accepted an addict like Alain only because of the dazzling recommendation of an extremely rich lady.

Besides, Alain himself had immediately aroused the

collector in him—the doctor saw the young man as a
splenetic dandy of the race of Chateaubriand and
Constant, as well as a specimen, to be examined at
close range at last, of that mysterious phenomenon,
today's youth. Yet Alain frightened him all the more
on this account: he trembled for fear that Alain would
suddenly do him some unsuspected harm. His huge,
fascinated eyes kept swiveling in his direction. He
sensed in this boy, for the moment so mild and polite,
all the dangerous forces which prowl through life and
society, and which he kept at a distance in this asylum
created first of all for himself—where he had unfortu-
nately trapped himself with his wife's frenzies. Alain
was almost always affable with him; the doctor was
grateful to him for it, but he was not reassured, and
perpetually feared seeing a flash of cruel mockery in
those deliberately lidded eyes. He had the vague feeling that Alain might say something that would humil-
iate him for a long time.

Despite his medical experience, he had persuaded
himself, for his own peace of mind, that Alain could,
without coercion, break his habit. In any case, he

counted heavily on the effects of a favorable emotional environment. This was why he had urged him to write to that American wife who, moreover, would be more likely than Alain to pay for the five weeks her husband had already spent in his establishment.

"Now look, my dear friend, just think for a minute. Your letter was sent a week ago. The answer couldn't have reached you yet."

Alain laughed derisively. The doctor, to avoid gloomy thoughts, looked forward to a future in which everything would come out all right. Everyone Alain knew treated him like this; they dodged the fact of his being.

"I tell you she couldn't believe my letter. When I married her, two years ago, I promised her I would never touch drugs again. I wasn't completely addicted then. And I kept my promise for several months; I drank. And then, she watched me go back to them."

"But now you're on the right track."

"You know this is my third try."

"The others weren't serious."

"I've never done anything serious."

"But you've learned a great deal. You see now
where it all leads."

"Yes. I'd rather die later than dry up and blow away
now."

"You know temptation inside out, you can't be taken
in any longer. Besides, you told me yourself, drugs no
longer have any effect on you, no longer amuse you."

Alain shrugged. It was all true and perfectly useless.

The first time, he had tried drugs for no particular
reason: a little hustler he was sleeping with took
cocaine; the following year, a friend was smoking . . .
He went back to them more and more often; he had
those nights to fill up; he was always alone; he was too
casual to have a regular mistress. Alcohol soon failed
to satisfy him and led back to drugs. And he kept
finding himself involved with the same group of idlers.
The kind who begin taking drugs because they have
nothing to do and continue because there's nothing
they can do.

He had discovered heroin, by which he had been
surprised and seduced. In fact, for a while he had

believed in a paradise on earth. Now that ephemeral illusion made him shrug his shoulders.

He had had his first heart seizure; one night he had fallen down, rigid, at a friend's house. That was when he had left for America. He had continued, nevertheless, in New York, where there were just as many temptations as in Paris. But there wasn't yet a complete regularity in his habit, he could still stand breaks; and when he had met Dorothy, he had been able, for several months, to pay her the homage of an almost complete abstinence.

But he had relapsed, and suddenly he had sensed a new kind of hold over his being, an inexorable grip. Obligatory regularity, increased frequency, larger doses. He had begun to be afraid, especially because Dorothy had abandoned him during a trip to Europe, and this had suddenly made him see drugs as an agent completely independent of his will, an agent making life impossible for him in every way.

That was when he had tried to break his habit according to the prescribed ritual, by going to a sanitarium. There he had discovered the sense of his utter collapse. Among madmen, under the thumb of doctors and orderlies, he had relapsed into his earliest servitudes: schoolroom and barracks. He had had to acknowledge himself a child, or die.

And, having reached the abstract and illusory point of the cure, that is, when his intake was down to zero, he finally realized what the habit meant. Although he seemed to be physically separated from drugs, all their effects remained within his being. Narcotics had changed the color of his life, and though they seemed to have gone, that color persisted. Whatever life drugs had left now seemed impregnated with them and drew him back to them. He could not make a gesture, pronounce a word, go somewhere, meet someone, without an association of ideas leading him back to drugs. All of his gestures resembled that of injecting himself (for he had taken heroin in solution): the very sound of his own voice could no longer awaken anything within him but his fate. He had been touched by death, drugs were death, he could not, from death, return to life. He could only plunge deeper into death, and so go back to drugs. This is the sophistry drugs inspire to justify relapse: I am lost, therefore I can take drugs again.

Finally, he suffered physically. This suffering was great; but, even if it had been less, it would still have been terrible for a man whose many acts of cowardice had long since conspired together to keep him in the absolute evasion of an artificial paradise. He had no defense against pain. Accustomed to yielding to the sensation of the moment, incapable of conceiving a life in which good and evil, pleasure and pain balanced and compensated for each other, he had not resisted for long the moral panic that physical suffering caused him. And he took drugs again.

But now, the stages of addiction he passed through again seemed different—lusterless. At each phase of his fall, he saw what a tawdry trap it had been. This was no longer the pleasure of a lie one recognizes but tolerates beneath the seductive mask of novelty; now, an overworked demon had hooked yet another client and mechanically repeated the idiotic old ruse: "If you take a little today, you'll take less tomorrow."

He who had complained of the monotony of his days rediscovered it on the one shortcut that had seemed to lead out of them.

He had had to acknowledge once and for all the

narrow limits within which drugs operate. It was simply a matter of physical tonality—more or less high, more or less low, like the effects of food and good health. "I'm full" or "I'm not full." It was to this completely digestive alternative that sensations reduced themselves. Through his mind passed only the most banal ideas, all derived from daily life, swathed in a false frivolity. He no longer had that spurting humor which, long before drugs, had come with his first disappointments, still less that florescence of alluring daydreams which, at sixteen, had afforded him a brief season of youth.

Finally, during a summer when he had not been able to take a swim or even stay long in the open air, he had seen clearly the true characteristics of the addict's life: dutiful, tidy, stay-at-home. The petty existence of the annuity-holder who lives with the shades drawn, hiding from adventures and problems. A routine of old maids united in a common piety, chaste, sour, gossipy, who turn away scandalized when aspersions are cast on their religion.

Terror, disgust, a vestige of vitality, the desire to repossess himself in order to win Lydia or win back

Dorothy and, with one or the other, money—all this permitted him a supreme mustering of forces. Whence this last attempt at a cure which was ending in Doctor de la Barbinais's sanitarium.

"You know, you don't look as disturbed as you did a few days ago. Do you still have those anxiety attacks?"

"I don't have anxiety *attacks*, I have *anxiety*. All the time."

"If you hold out for a little while longer, it will gradually ease off."

Alain turned his eyes away from the hypocrite. He knew that the doctor, blinded as he was by fear, possessed at least the elementary knowledge of an ordinary practitioner; therefore he was lying through his teeth. How could he talk about holding out when the disease attacked the very core of the will?

And here, in fact, is the enormous stupidity of our times: the doctor appeals to his patient's will while his doctrine denies the existence of that will, declares it to be determined, divided between various determining factors. Individual will is the myth of another age; a race exhausted by civilization cannot believe in the will. Perhaps it will take refuge in constraint: the rising tyrannies of fascism and communism promise to flagellate the addicts.

"A strong, healthy woman like these Americans will make you forget all this," the doctor repeated meaningfully.

Alain ended by nodding acquiescence: a man cannot continually sustain the lucidity that shows him the final consequences of his habits. He falls back into the chiaroscuro of the everyday, where he counter-balances the progress of his acts with hopes and illusions. This is why Alain still returned for long periods to the idea he had cherished all through his youth—a youth that was coming to an end, for he had just turned thirty, and thirty is a lot for a boy with nothing in his favor but his looks—the idea that everything would be taken care of by women.

At that moment, the dim sense of defeat produced by Lydia's departure led him back to Dorothy.

"You know what you ought to do, my friend," the doctor continued, "you ought to cable your wife. By now she's received your letter, which certainly touched her. But you must reinforce her conviction, make her believe you'll persevere."

"What for?" Alain murmured.

Yet the idea appealed to him. He had always enjoyed telegrams, in which he satisfied his taste for a
disastrous humor and also his easily abridged impulses of tenderness.

"Listen to me. Cable her; tell her to take the first
boat. Stay here until she arrives; then as soon as she
gets here, go south with her, or even farther. Above
all, don't go to Paris, don't go back to those people
who are ruining your life."

"What's one telegram more or less? It won't be my
first, or my last," he exclaimed.

Then he continued, to himself: "My last, yes, probably my last."

Nevertheless, the doctor sensed that he had scored
a point; he tried to profit from his advantage.

"Since at the moment you're in good shape, all in
all, you should do something about your business as
well."

"Business." Alain almost laughed in his face. Yet
there were illusions here, too, out of which he made
his daily bread.

The doctor respected Alain's preposterous tastes.

Admiring spontaneously only the eccentrics of the past, from Byron to Jarry, he vaguely realized that the perspective of time helped him praise things that at close range would have disconcerted him as they had the vulgar herd of Baudelaire's contemporaries. And, so as never to be caught off guard, he avoided censuring anything his own epoch offered.

He stood up and once again gazed longingly at the ornaments on the mantelpiece. He would have liked to admire them all, but could not manage it; yet the fact that he was able to keep his eyes on these disconcerting objects for a moment seemed a result with which he was soon content.

"Your idea of a shop sounds excellent. You must get started right away. All those things will amuse many people."

Among other delusory projects, Alain had thought of opening a shop in Paris or New York to sell all those dated, ugly, or absurd objects which industry, hovering between the popular and the vulgar, has produced in the last fifty years, and which had become a fad in the twenties, reviving and violating the much earlier tastes of certain artists. So Alain had thought of selling at high prices a whole eccentric farrago: flea circuses, collections of sentimental or obscene postcards, *images d'Epinal,* glass balls, boats in bottles, wax figures, etc. . . .

But he needed capital to finance the project. To whom could he turn? Alain had alienated all his friends. He ran through some vague possibilities, but without attempting to give them any reality. For example, why not interest Mademoiselle Farnoux in his fate? But Mademoiselle Farnoux never spent all her income, and kept good works to a minimum: a radical journal, two or three Russian émigrés, and a few old retainers she had grown tired of.

Besides, Alain was afraid that this vogue, already several years old, would pass, for he failed to understand that in our composite age, nothing passes and all old fads continue to live, one on top of the other. There are still devotees of the Renaissance and the eighteenth century as well as collectors of Negro masks and cubist painters, while others hunt down the debris of Art Nouveau or Second Empire. Thus Alain could have gone merrily on, but he was not crude enough for that.

"For example," the doctor continued, warming to the idea, "you ought to make collages like the one on the mirror. Those are plates of psychological illustrations, just as there are entomological ones."

Alain suddenly laughed. The doctor turned around in alarm and saw what he had been dreading for so long: Alain's regular features were twisted into a grin, the deceptive health the cure had given to his features was scored and dented by nervous twitches that revealed, below the surface, the emaciating action of the drugs.

"You don't like my idea?"

"No."

"What a strange boy you are! Well, I see I'm tiring you; I'll be on my way."

"Yes, I must dress, I'm going out."

"You're going out again?"

"Yes, I have to cash a check."

"Oh! That's different . . . Still, you could wait. Besides, it's too late."

"I know it is, but I also have to meet someone . . . about the shop, in fact."

"And you'll be gone all night again?"

"No, of course not."

Alain didn't bother pretending, and even as he said no he indicated yes. He resented the doctor's indulgence that left open the door to death, and by his defiance he sought to force the old man to the point of complicity.

The doctor sensed this challenge and was very disturbed by it; for, in this peaceful asylum, he had never been coerced into exercising authority. The fear of something bad happening to Alain might have given him the courage, but even more than Alain's temerity he feared his irony. He dared not protest that life was good, for he felt he possessed no convincing arguments.

Suddenly, without looking at him, he touched Alain's hand and fled.

4   ALAIN, AFTER DRAWING THE CURTAINS AND turning on the lights, began to dress for the evening. He still enjoyed foraging in the wardrobe left over from the good days, when Dorothy and he, in Florida and on the Côte d'Azur, had run through the settlement her first husband had made on her.

A man who lives alone is an illusionist. In Miami or Monte Carlo, Alain, standing in front of a trunk full of expensive clothes, would try on a new tie while smoking a cigarette. His bottles, his brushes, a dressing-gown trailing on the bed illuminated the drab hotel room with luxury. His pockets were full of dollars; the night would expand . . . wines would flow, men and women alike would succumb to his charm.

Drugs, which isolated him from all contacts, which

kept him from ever having to prove himself, had
trapped him in this motionless fantasy.

He chose a batiste shirt, a cashmere suit, rough
woolen socks: all the same shade of gray. And a tie
with a red background—one he had stolen from his
friend Dubourg: he used to think he stole things as a
joke, but now he knew it was covetousness. And he
got out shoes of heavy leather, with crudely stitched
seams. An elegance discreet enough to be indecipher-
able.

He was not hurrying. On the contrary, he made
each gesture deliberate, sharpening his desire.

But this desire was so abstract it could almost satisfy itself. His debauch would be purely mental. His
appropriation of the world would reduce itself to a
single gesture, and that gesture would not reach out to
things. He would barely move his arm from his body,
and would immediately draw it back: to thrust a
needle under the skin. And yet the habits of hope and
confidence that make up the warp of life are so strong
that he would attempt to embellish this gesture. He
would try—he would go toward people, he would
speak to them as if he expected something from them,

as if he wanted to share life with them. But, in fact, nothing of the sort would happen. Contrary to vulgar superstition, phantoms are as ineffectual as they are intangible.

He slowed down his desire until it began to lose direction.

Half-dressed, he took out of the cupboard, from between two shirts, a pretty little case in which the syringe had been sleeping for several weeks. He turned it in his fingers for a minute or two. He put it back, afraid. Just now he had desperately committed himself to his inclination, though he was quite sure where this final relapse would lead. He got his revolver from the trunk, and placed it beside the syringe. The two belonged together.

Yet he had not spent the days of his youth in such pursuits.

In those days, he used to talk about suicide. But murder fondled in such fashion was a free, voluntary act; now, an alien and stupid power had appropriated that unmotivated vow, which had been no more, perhaps, than an explosion of fierce vitality, and this power was pushing him down the monotonous corridor of disease toward a slow death. And sensing this humiliating change of control, he had lingered in his final asylum. He had remained—motionless, fragile, fearing to make the slightest gesture, knowing that whatever it was, it would be his death sentence.

And now he was making that gesture in spite of himself: he was going out, he was already knotting his tie. He lowered his hands to see himself more clearly in the mirror, leaning over it as if it were the circle of a well. The collage got in his way, he tore the pieces off. Still water. He would have liked to attach his image to that apparent immobility, gluing there his being threatened with an immanent dissolution.

That dissolution was already far advanced. At eighteen, Alain's regular features had had a certain beauty. That beauty had seemed a promise which intoxicated him. He could remember the reactions of women when he entered a room. In the broad structure of his face, there was something infrangible that he gloated over the morning after a night's debauchery. For a long time it had given him a sense of immunity. But today . . . True, the bones were still in place, but even they seemed corroded, like a steel carcass warped and twisted by fire. The straight ridge of his nose had arched; pinched between two hollows, it seemed about to break. The once decisive line of his chin, which had offered such a sure challenge, no longer managed to assert itself against the flesh into which it vanished. Nor were his eye sockets clearly defined between temples and cheekbones. Something unhealthy had spread through all his tissues and had tainted them, even his eyeballs. But that yellow fat, the laborious product of the cure, was still too much life, too much being; the slightest grin, the slightest grimace brought back those terrible hollows, those terrible emaciations that a year or two before had begun to carve a death mask out of the living substance. He surmised, ready to reappear, those gray shadows that had wasted him so terribly up until the preceding July.

And in the mirror, he stared over his shoulder. That empty room, that solitude . . . A terrible shudder seized the pit of his loins, the marrow of his bones, and ran like icy lightning from his feet to his head: death was an absolute presence. This was solitude; he had threatened life with it as with a knife, and now that knife had turned and was piercing his entrails. There was no one left, no hope left. An irreparable isolation. Dorothy was in New York, she had tossed his letter into the fire and gone off dancing with a rich, healthy, reliable man who protected her, who possessed her. Lydia was on the ship, surrounded by gigolos. The shudder grew still more intense when he thought of that ship plunging like a nutshell in the horrible November night, in the horrible black basin, lashed by polar winds.

His friends? Those who were like himself waited, laughing derisively, for him to fall back among them; the others had turned their backs, drawn away, absorbed by their incredible love of life. His parents? He had long since accustomed them to disbelieve in his existence. Even when he was still living with them, they had sensed his withdrawal, for all the show of tenderness he offered. They had watched him retreat with fierce discretion from all the ideas and habits that seemed to them the guarantees of existence. He had refused to take his baccalaureate examination, had calmly scorned any trade or profession, and went on asking them for money, never a tremendous amount, but insistently, and always for a little more than they could afford, until the time came when they had had to refuse for good. Then he had plunged, without once turning back, into a suspect world where to them everything seemed strange, inhuman, evil. And when he occasionally came to see them, they had no words, no feelings for this shadow abominably alienated from the land of the living, this stranger who looked at them with the distant, derisive tenderness of a dead man.

And so he would have to die alone, in the cold paroxysm of drugs.

He opened a drawer and took out the photographs of Dorothy and Lydia to exorcise that solitude by images, as a believer touches an icon. But he did not look long at the picture of Lydia.

He had met Dorothy too late. She was the lovely, kind, rich woman all his weaknesses required; but these weaknesses were already consummated. He had waited too long.

He had not learned to fling himself on women from the first, to make sure of them while they still wanted him. He had kept the habit of his adolescence, to wait for them, to watch them from a distance. Until he was twenty-five, when he still possessed vigorous health and a strikingly handsome appearance, he had had only short affairs, and withdrew immediately, discouraged by a word or a gesture, suddenly afraid he was no longer giving pleasure, or taking it, tempted by the momentary diversion of a farcical exit which would be followed, beyond the door, by a paroxysm of bitterness. So that he had no experience of women's hearts nor of his own, and still less of bodies.

When he went to New York, the mirages reappeared. And he suddenly had greater success. A Frenchwoman, whether she is a whore or not, wants to be taken, wants to be kept. In exchange, she is ready to give herself utterly: a prudent and profitable exchange. Alain had been frightened by these demands for tenderness and sensuality. On the contrary, an American woman, when she is not looking for a husband, is more easily satisfied by a thoughtless liaison. Badly educated, forward, generous, she seems almost indifferent to the quality of what is offered in an affair. Alain, moreover, with the help of alcohol and drugs, had grown bolder as a result of these off-hand contacts. But he had not learned much from them.

So that when he met Dorothy, his confusion had been great.

Especially since one other thing kept him at a distance from women: his idea of money. Quite naturally attracted by luxury, he constantly found himself in the company of rich women, and kept assuring himself that part of their charm was, in fact, their money. In the invincible isolation he was sinking into, this idea had grown more and more overpowering.

It became an unendurable torment in the case of Dorothy, with whom he had fallen in love: she was gentle, good to him. His scruples were betrayed by an atrocious irony he turned against himself.

"I love you, you must be rich," he had told her one evening.

She had answered very seriously, "It's too bad I'm not rich enough. I'm sorry."

She did not understand Alain's bitterness at all, for she had never known a society where money was not taken for granted. The fathers have worked for it, but the sons or daughters don't remember that, and to them it seems only natural that those of their friends and relatives who happen not to be rich should become so by the only means conceivable: by marriage.

Her attitude was sustained by Alain's disdainful pose of being an aristocrat to whom all privileges were due. Considering herself less intelligent and less refined than he, she regarded her wealth as her only legitimate attraction. She asked his forgiveness for not having more, she wanted to shower him with gold. And in fact, she spent on him all that she had not squandered of the money settled on her by her first husband, who was quite rich, and then a part of her inheritance from her father.

Yet, Alain had no great need of money. Like most of the bourgeoisie, he aspired to a financial level only just above the one he had known in his childhood. He had incurred, up till now, only small debts. But he had a false reputation to maintain, and he had not wanted to lag behind his wife when it came to spending. And they had done so well, the two of them, that they soon found themselves in straitened circumstances. Which had added considerably to their other difficulties.

Dorothy understood nothing of the irony Alain lavished on himself, on his motives; she believed he despised himself for loving her, a girl who had neither wit nor imagination. She had supposed he would be pleased with her modest attitude. Yet Alain took her humility for an affectation, a cunning reply to his ulterior motives: she was pretending to hide behind her money since it was her money he resented. He supposed he had been judged, and his bitterness mounted.

He might have overcome these misunderstandings, if he had been able to establish a sensual intimacy between them, but he had not. This rake was ignorant, and the feeling of his ignorance made him timid; he panicked before Dorothy's modesty, which was nothing but apprehension, the fault of her first husband who had been brutal with her and forced her back into a virginal somnolence. Alain took her in his arms with an awkwardness that suddenly revealed to him the incredible poverty of his life. He did not know what to do, because he had never done anything. He lay whole nights beside her, shivering with misery. Of course she was his wife, but for such fugitive, distracted moments. He needed to burst into tears, to wrench an immense and sordid confession from himself; he could not do it. So he became irritable, he ground his teeth. And this was the reason he went back to drugs, trying to forget in them the shame that overwhelmed him.

Little by little Dorothy grew terrified. She realized she had been despoiled, with nothing to show for it. After two or three false starts which had collapsed in reawakened tenderness and pity, she managed to escape.

And Alain had lost the great opportunity of his life, for the drugs which had regained control of him deadened all his apprehensions and also incited him to nourish new and vague hopes about Lydia, who had appeared on the scene at this point.

But now he knew Dorothy's value. Deep within himself, he believed he still had some power over her and that he could win her back, if he only took the trouble. And he couldn't believe she failed to share his feelings. She looked so kind, in the photograph. Her mouth echoed her eyes: a timid tenderness. Her delicate breasts repeated the same thing, and her yielding skin, her slender hands.

He had to cable her. He didn't want death as it loomed now, he didn't want to come apart fiber by fiber.

He tore off his tie and shirt, wrapped himself in his bathrobe, and sat down at the table. He took a sheet of paper and laid it in front of him with all the care he lavished on the rare gestures that represented his last hold on life, and with the timid deliberation of those who do not have the habit of writing.

He began making rough drafts.

Cable reply, need you. Minutes count.

No, not that, too tragic.

You have a lover in Paris.

Nor that, after everything that had happened. He remembered an evening, during one of their stays in Paris, when he had gone out alone and dashed into a brothel in search of a chimerical recompense for the abstraction of his married life. When he returned, she had stayed in his room while he undressed, and this is what had struck her like a slap in the face: on each of her husband's breasts, a lipsticked kiss.

The memory was so scathing that it dissipated his impulse. Discouraged, he put down his pen and went back to thinking about the drugs that were waiting for him in Paris.

Yet the blank paper still demanded his attention.

Await your letter with patience and hope.

It was flat, it sounded too careful, too composed. He decided to leave it at that. And he copied the words onto another sheet with a sense of relief.

In his whole life, Alain had never made a gesture that indicated so prolonged a pursuit of the same goal. And all at once, from this paper where this gesture had crystallized, there emanated a power. For a long moment, there had been something in his life, and he was going to rebuild everything around that thing. Cling, rebuild, cling . . .

He got up, rang the bell. The maid came and he handed her the precious telegram. With a feverish, excessive insistence, he instructed her to take it to the cable office immediately, and he gave her the rest of

the hundred francs he had borrowed from the door-
man that morning to pay for his taxi.

Then he returned to his table, fascinated. He had
glimpsed the potency of writing, whose meshes ceaselessly gather and combine all the diffuse forces of
human life. He opened the locked briefcase with a
little key he kept in his pocket. Inside lay several
manuscript pages. On one of them was written: *The
Ticketless Traveler.* It was the sketch of a confession,
reduced to a few uncertain lines which frayed out into
the margins of the sheet. A sentence, a paragraph, a
word. He turned the pages; he suffered less than usual
from that fear and that inhibition which always paralyzed him in the act of writing. He had never realized
that even if his soul had not been bled white, he could
not hope to tap it without first coercing it, contracting
and constraining it with pain and effort.

He reread several pages—which began briskly,
hesitated, dribbled out. He saw the places where they
faltered; and a little of what needed to be incorpo-
rated into that thin text trembled within him.

He picked up his pen, hesitated, took courage,
touched the paper, marked it. An affecting moment:

Alain was approaching life. He had been taught, in
certain literary circles he had once frequented, to dis-
trust literature. In that attitude he had found a line of
least resistance which suited his frivolity, his laziness.
Moreover, rejecting life as he did, he could not imagine anything *except* what he called, with a justifiable
scorn, *literature*—that purposeless exercise which absorbed the energy of those very people who had inspired his scorn. He could not conceive a profound
and compelling sort of investigation in which a man
turns to art to discover his own sense of direction, his
own characteristics. And now, without wanting to,
without knowing it, by an instinctive leap, he had
taken the path that led directly to the grave mysteries
he had always avoided. Since he was experiencing the
unforeseen benefits to be derived from writing, he
might have been able, henceforth, to grasp its func-
tion: to create an ordered universe in which the writer
can live. For the first time in his life, he was putting a
semblance of order into his feelings, and he immediately began to breathe a little, no longer choked by
those feelings which were not complex, but so tangled, so tightly knotted because they had never been

articulated. Would he not realize that it had been
wrong to give up, to declare, without having ever
really looked, that the world is nothing, that it has no
substance?

But he tired quickly. He had completed two or
three pages—more than he had ever written before at
one sitting. The little caravan of words, bearing the
light baggage of desires (which might have supplied
him with a reason for living), had been abandoned so
long in the desert of paper that he had barely got it
underway again before it faltered and collapsed once
more in that white wasteland.

He put down his pen and promised himself to return to it tomorrow. Then all of a sudden he gave a
start and looked at his watch: it was seven o'clock. He
was able to convince himself it was too late to go into
Paris. His center of gravity was so readily displaced
that he could keep himself where he was. He decided
to go to bed, to have his dinner on a tray, and then to
read a little.

His friend Dubourg telephoned, and Alain delight-
edly accepted an invitation to lunch for the next day.

5   THE NEXT MORNING, AROUND ELEVEN
thirty, in a little bar on the route de Quarante-Sous,
two delivery men from the Galeries Lafayette had
parked their big yellow truck and were having a drink.

A gentleman came in, all in gray.

He was well dressed, but there was something
funny about his expression; he looked sick, almost. It
made you uncomfortable to look at him, yet nothing
seemed actually wrong.

He asked for English cigarettes. There weren't any.

"You should keep them in stock," Alain said in a
friendly but rather strained voice.

"Nobody asks for them around here."

"I did."

"One time isn't enough, the merchandise gets stale."

"I'd have taken all you had. Still, you couldn't know I was coming. Give me a Pernod."

Funny conversation, the men at the bar thought. Alain went over to the bar and glanced at them vaguely while his drink was being poured. He downed it in one gulp and asked for another. Then he turned to the delivery men.

"Are you going back to Paris?"

"Yes."

"Will you give me a ride?"

"It's not allowed."

"I know. But have a drink with me anyway. Bartender, two more."

He clinked glasses with them, then they took him in the truck with them.

What would he do in Paris? Have lunch with Dubourg. Was that all? Cash his check. Afterward? Afterward . . .

Waking this morning, he had stared from his bed at the papers on the table. But last night's excitement was gone, his enthusiasm dead. He had immediately decided to stop writing, to stop thinking. And he had justified this change by his appointment with Dubourg: it was late, he only had time to get dressed. He sneaked out, avoiding the doctor.

The two delivery men were intimidated by Alain, even a little afraid of him, for to them he seemed to be following strange and dangerous paths.

"You work around here?" one of them asked.

"I don't work."

"You live off an income?"

"No."

Alain gave these abrupt answers in a cordial tone, in which the delivery men could detect no trace of mockery.

"I'm sick."

"Oh! That's it."

"That's what?"

"Well, you don't look so good."

"You mean I look terrible."

"Maybe you were gassed."

"Gassed? Yes, I've been gassed."

"That's tough. But sometimes you get over it. A buddy of mine got it at Montdidier . . ."

"Let's not talk about the war."

The delivery man immediately fell silent.

All friendliness had disappeared from Alain's face. "They're all alike," he murmured.

"Huh?" asked the one who hadn't said anything.

"Oh nothing! Doesn't it bother you not to have money?"

"Well, sure!"

"It bothers me."

"Sure, if you don't work, you can't make money."

The delivery men looked questioningly at Alain's clothes.

"You'd be surprised if I told you I was as poor as you, that I'm stone broke."

"You look like you're doing all right."

"I just look like that."

The delivery man didn't labor the point, and he wasn't offended, for Alain's mockery was obviously directed at himself.

At the gates of Paris, Alain got out, after giving them twenty francs. He had extracted another hundred francs from the sanitarium concierge by waving the check in his face.

They drove on, pleased and troubled.

Alain jumped into a taxi and drove straight to Bankers Trust, where he leafed through ten crisp thousand-franc notes. Out of habit, he stopped in at the Ritz bar, where he drank a martini among the rich young Americans and the big-time crooks. Then he took a taxi to Dubourg's.

Dubourg lived in a little apartment on the rue Guénégaud, on the top floor of an old house. Despite the electricity and the steam heat that penetrated the old carcass, the structure was evidently rotten to the core. Alain shuddered on the great staircase, where stale smells lingered and the light trembled in the shadows.

An old Negress came to the door, which creaked when she opened it. Then he was in the heart of this bright, small apartment crammed with books, standing over Dubourg, who as usual was stretched out on the striped sofa, amid an accumulation of papers, his pipe between his teeth, a pen in his hand. A young girl squatted beside him, watching him write. Dubourg threw down his pen, pushed the papers aside, and stood up. He was quite tall and thin, his bald skull surmounting a child's face blurred by the approach of his fortieth year.

He held out his hand to Alain with a mixture of joy and anxiety that made him clumsy.

"I certainly am glad to see *you!* How are you?"

"Oh, all right . . . Hello, Faveur."

Alain embraced the girl, who stood beside her father, already tall and thin like him; she accepted the kiss with quiet enjoyment.

"Faveur, run along now."

She had already disappeared. Dubourg looked at Alain, looked around the room, looked back at Alain, and shook his head. Alain's eyes followed Dubourg's distractedly.

Dubourg had become an Egyptologist not long before, soon after his marriage. With a certain irony, Alain had watched the former companion of his drinking bouts mend his ways. What defeat had he sought in these papyri? What was he doing with a wife and two daughters? What did this crowded solitude mean?

Yet friendship was the only aperture through which any tenderness could enter Alain's heart. Alain, whose

imperious nature considered any mixture of good
evil as life's ultimate insult to himself, somehow accepted the fact that Dubourg got only a little of what
he wanted by putting up with a great deal of what he
didn't. Dubourg had virtues—he never loaned money,
he gave it; his lies were transparent; and it was with
an unalloyed tenderness that he maligned his friends.
But he was a pharisee. If he didn't have the manners
of one, he concealed deep in his heart the usual fund
of imbecilic reservations: not God, but the love of life
generated his bigotry.

And, as always, he did everything in his power to
justify Alain's opinion of him; with his evasive glances
around the room, he seemed to be apologizing for this
peaceful existence he had nonetheless settled for.

But now he forced himself to look directly into
Alain's eyes and, leaning against the mantel, asked:
"How far along are you?"

"Oh . . ."

"When are you coming to stay here?"

"In a while."

Dubourg was appalled by Alain's addiction, and
never stopped thinking about a cure. In moments of

hope, Alain was touched by his friend's solicitude and tried to emulate Dubourg's interest in his recovery. He had promised his friend he would come and live on the rue Guénégaud, like a convict released from prison who attempts to give his old instincts the slip. But Dubourg feared his friend's prejudices against him, and instead of confronting him head on, wasted his time trying to avoid offending him.

"You'll sleep here," he suggested.

The room was attractive. Light poured in over the roofs of the Mint. Narrow and very high-ceilinged, it was painted a flat white. The carpet was cream-colored, pale in contrast to the book bindings, some native fabrics, flowers. But it was all steeped in the sweetish riddle of Dubourg's life.

"Are you afraid of leaving . . . that place?" continued Dubourg, who noticed the face Alain had made.

"Yes."

Dubourg's wife entered, interrupting these timid overtures. She was a tall, thin girl with languid inflections, quite naked beneath her dress. Beautiful hair, beautiful eyes, bad teeth. She was accompanied by her two daughters—the second just like the first—and a cat. The little troupe made no noise. Dubourg said he had married Fanny because of her extraordinary aptitude for silence and horizontality. "When we're alone, you can't hear a sound in the house. She's lying down in her room, I'm on the couch here—only the children stand up." Their listlessness made his account more than likely.

Alain kissed Fanny's hand ceremoniously. Dubourg watched with incredulity, convinced that no one besides himself could notice the existence of a woman who was not pretty and who expressed herself only in secret transports.

With a gesture, she indicated that lunch was served, and they went into a room where a table was set, surrounded by stools. As in the neighboring room, the carpet was very thick. The walls were covered with light fabrics, decorated here and there by Coptic embroideries with bright, delicate patterns.

During the meal, which consisted of two exotic dishes, both light and subtle, and fruit, only Alain and Dubourg spoke. Fanny, Faveur, and the other girl, whose name Alain did not remember, listened with

expressions of repressed pleasure. Alain felt surrounded by an insinuating spell, a discreet conspir-
acy: even the cat joined the plot and rubbed against
him as though inadvertently.

Dubourg was afraid he would rebel against all this
domesticity, and tried to divert him. He told stories
about the past, but Alain, who since turning thirty
had gorged himself on memories of himself at eighteen, could not endure the same sentimentality in
others. Yet Dubourg spoke with a rather humorous
detachment and offered only very brief anecdotes,
gaily told and abruptly dropped. He was trying to
draw comic effects from the rather brutal contrast
forming in Alain's mind between today's Dubourg and
the one of ten years ago.

When the war ended, Dubourg was already bald,
but still a dashing young man. His mistress gave him
quite a bit of money which he in turn gave to other
women. His apartment was always full of easygoing
girls and boys. They drank, and they made love. In
the summer they went to Spain, to Morocco. Dubourg
soon dropped his protectress; then he contracted a
liver disease and became indifferent to women in gen-

eral. Quite early, he had had second thoughts, apparently, and his friends reported finding him in bed, around noon, his back turned to his mistress, his nose buried in fat books on religious history. One day he paid his debts and asked Fanny to marry him; with a nod of her head she agreed. He left for Cairo, where she had been born, and now he lived immured in these absurd studies, almost poor, with the sweet vermin of a wife and children on his back.

The vermin disappeared after lunch and left the two men facing one another in the white study, supplied with coffee and tobacco. During lunch, Dubourg, as he was chatting, had sensed Alain's secret: it was fear. What was its source?

"How's it going?"

"Badly."

"Will you see it through?"

"What for? What the hell do you want from life?" Alain sat down on the sofa, among the hieroglyphics.

Dubourg remained standing, his pipe in his hand. Emotions welled up and propelled him toward his friend. In the past two years, he had found certainty, he lived in a state of perpetual enthusiasm. But it would have taken an enormous effort to sift everything personal out of this enthusiasm, so that, in letting it flow over Alain, it would not hurt or irritate him. He bitterly regretted not being farther along in his metamorphosis: one can give only what one has already assimilated. Dubourg was too honest, and Alain too acute, to pretend that this transformation was more advanced than it was and to attenuate all the neophyte's self-satisfaction still obvious in his eyes and his hands when he talked about his discoveries.

Alain sensed this repressed effusion and, not speaking, challenged his friend with a look. Then, the next second, he thought of his salvation, was terrified by Dubourg's ineffectualness and secretly reproached him for it.

Dubourg, however, decided to join combat.

"Listen, there are still things in life . . . well, you know!"

"My dear Dubourg . . ."

"A boy like you—I'd really like to see you doing something . . ."

"Doing something!"

"Yes, it's marvelous, doing something really well. There are things you could do wonderfully."

"What?"

"Well, I don't know. But after all, you must have your own idea of what you want from life. And it's impossible for it to just . . . disappear. I hate things being kept back; you have to let out what's inside you . . . It hurts me—you hurt me."

"I hurt you?"

"I'm not ashamed to say it."

"But letting out what I have inside me will only hurt you more."

Dubourg, having got started, passed over this threatening remark.

"What you can do, you'd do very well. You have charm, skill . . ."

Alain, leaning back on the hieroglyphics, shook his head. Dubourg continued to advance, feeling him out.

"Drugs aren't everything. You think that you and drugs are the same thing, but after all, you don't really know. It's like a foreign body. There's Alain, and then . . . Alain. Alain can change. Why do you want to keep the first skin you were born with?"

"To be the same. I've always been the same."

"Once you chose to be what you are today; you can stop being that and still be yourself, but in another way. I know you want to be a lot of things."

"I've thought of two or three things at once. I've never 'wanted' anything."

"I know you want at least four different things: women, money, friendship, and then . . . no, only three."

"I've never wanted anything except a little money, like everybody else."

"If that were true, you'd have worked for it, or stolen it. No, what you call money is the opposite of money, it's an excuse for daydreaming."

Dubourg stopped for a moment and indulged himself a little too obviously in the association of his thoughts. His eyes gleamed.

"Basically, you're a bourgeois."

"Please, let's not use words that don't mean anything."

"Explanations are only good for little things, I know . . . But at least they have the advantage of clearing those little things out of the way."

"Go on . . . I don't want to deprive you d pleasure."

"Alain my friend, you're mistaken. For a long time now psychology hasn't been enough for me; what I like about people isn't so much their passions but what comes *out* of their passions, something just as strong—ideas, gods. Gods are born with men and die with men, but those tangled tribes are part of eternity. All right, we won't talk about that . . . Look, this is the way I see it: you were born into an old *petit-bourgeois* family, and money was a little spring in the corner of the garden, used for watering the vegetables. Everyone had to keep busy—with himself! In other words, inheritance, sinecure, or marriage. Now you, even though you rebelled against your family, you quite naturally inherited this prejudice. You haven't surrendered to the times like most of the people we know; you haven't accepted the new law of forced labor, and you're still tied to the tradition of money that falls from heaven—money that turns you into a dreamer. That's what it is."

"Are you through?"

Dubourg lowered his head and drew on his pipe,

abashed. That wasn't at all what he had wanted to say. He should have gone much further, but it would have taken a long time, and despite the seriousness of the moment, he still feared Alain's mockery.

"You think these explanations are useless. But you'll agree that in your imagination money has always had an importance out of all proportion to your real desire for it."

Alain did not answer, he was getting bored. Dubourg took a long time to relight his pipe.

"Then there's the sun," he began again suddenly.

That was better. For an instant, Dubourg seemed luminous to Alain as he remembered that horrible summer when he saw himself, in bright sunlight, exiled to a world of darkness. Drugs had thrown their shadow over his face, his hands; he felt the dusk in his eyes.

"You ought to come with us to Egypt this winter."

Dubourg wrapped himself in a cloud of smoke and looked up more boldly at Alain. He remembered that he had settled his accounts: he liked meat, vegetables, fruit, tobacco. Once he had been befuddled by irony, but now he let his liking spread to all the forms of Nature and Society. This love of forms led him to worship the gods of Egypt and at the same time endure his vermin of a family.

"Come with us to Egypt, the people there have the sun in their bellies."

Dubourg was still not pleased with himself. He had found nothing direct or penetrating to say. He was beating around the bush. He returned to the attack, but feebly, repeating himself.

"You're funny, Dubourg, when you're trying to be nice."

Alain watched him flinch, and despised him for not asserting himself: perhaps he wanted to be attacked. The past summer, Dubourg had written him a scorching letter: "I wonder how I can ever forgive you for lying to me the way you always do. Every time you leave the room to give yourself a shot, you tell me you're going to pee." A sentence like that had driven him to the sanitarium.

Dubourg had felt himself faltering, and sensed that Alain had noticed it; he swallowed hard. "Listen, I'm not the only one. There are people who live in a big-ger world than I do—what they *say* might have more of an effect on you."

Dubourg despaired of making Alain understand that from the moment he had seemed to be living less, he was living more. He would have liked to offer ex-amples easier to comprehend than his own. Examples full of the open air, of brute force. But at the same time, it outraged him that Alain had no idea of the powers of the inner life, did not realize that they gleam in the sun as brightly as heroic adventures. He would have liked to recite some of those Egyptian prayers distended with the fullness of being, in which the spiritual life, exploding, pours out all the sap of the earth. He was growing impatient, and the objurga-tions on his lips were already turning to sarcasm: "Don't blame your poverty on life." But that would drive Alain straight into nothingness, into hell.

Yet what he said was: "Listen, you're wrong about me, don't judge by appearances. You think you're looking at a *petit-bourgeois* sellout. But I live more intensely then I ever did when I was just getting drunk and sleeping around. Eventually I'll write a book with all the power of Egypt in it. It's in my blood already. And it will flow from my veins into others. It will help people."

Alain shrugged his shoulders. He nursed two contradictory prejudices against Dubourg: on the one hand, he resented his optimism—optimism, for Alain, was identified with vulgarity or hypocrisy; on the other, his view of life—for him it could only be action, not thought. It never occurred to Alain that life could originate in backwaters like this apartment on the rue Guénégaud.

So he could not help replying: "You don't seem so pleased with the life you're leading now."

As Alain expected, Dubourg immediately winced. If he was strongly attached to ideas, he was not so attached to himself; and to that degree he betrayed his ideas.

"That doesn't matter," he mumbled. "What does is the thought that passes through me."

"But you're in a rut."

"Fanny and the girls and this rickety old house are all part of my passion."

"Your eyes don't shine the way they used to."

"I'm older."

"Then all you're telling me . . ."

"No, I haven't grown old. I'm no longer a young man, but I'm not old. I'm much more alive than I used to be. Your problem is that you won't let go of your youth and start another life. I have no more hope, but I have certainty. Aren't you tired of mirages? Basically, you don't need any more money than I do."

"I loathe mediocrity."

"For the last ten years, you've been living in nothing but a gilded mediocrity. The worst kind."

"Exactly, and I'm fed up with it."

"So?"

Dubourg immediately regretted this exclamation; it was frightening to ask Alain final questions.

"If I go back to drugs, I'll kill myself."

"I'll keep you from going back. What are you going to do in a month when you leave here, when you're really back on your feet?"

Dubourg made an effort to speak these confident words with assurance.

Alain dared not mention his plan for a shop.

"Go into business. I have some ideas."

Despite his fear of discouraging Alain, Dubourg continued to speak frankly, hoping to clear the air.

"Listen. It has to be one thing or the other: do you want freedom or money? If you want money, you have to start over, get a job at two thousand francs a month and work at it. If you don't, then go back to Dorothy—you can live on the hundred thousand francs a year she's still got. You can have a little apartment like this one, and see friends, and rediscover your mind: you've forgotten about it the last two or three years."

Alain made a face. Dubourg was surprised, then annoyed. What was at the root of all Alain's despair?

"Alain, if you had married five hundred thousand francs a year, would you be happy?"

A suicidal look came into Alain's eyes. Dubourg was appalled. He wanted to make another attempt to get under Alain's skin, to grasp his secret reason for living, to caress it, to make it bloom.

"Listen, Alain, Dorothy's a lovely woman and you're the most attractive man I know. Do your friends a favor and go back to her. You were made to be loved and taken care of by a beautiful woman. At least a few people should be able to escape this horrible compulsion to work."

But this could only hurt Alain: he had so little faith in his talent with women that he suspected Dubourg of faking this confidence in him.

"You know I have very little influence over women."

Dubourg had not been faking, but he immediately began to wonder, and his eyes showed his curiosity. Yet he said: "What nonsense!"

"Women used to go wild over my pretty face when I was twenty. Now they think I'm nice. But that's not enough."

"What?"

Alain looked at Dubourg with annoyance.

"Why do you pretend you don't know? There's nothing sensual about me."

"You just imagine that."

"I don't believe in missed vocations."

"Yet you're tortured by the thought of women."

"I have little effect on them, but even so, it's only through women I have any effect on things. For me, women have always meant money."

"Don't give me that. You wouldn't stay five minutes

with a woman you didn't love. I've never seen you when you weren't in love. You still love Dorothy, right now."

"But you'll notice I've always been in love with rich women."

"Dorothy isn't so rich."

"She isn't poor either."

Dubourg was still perplexed. "So that's your problem. You can't love a woman without money; and you can't love a woman with money either, because you have to love her money along with her."

"Maybe . . ."

"And drugs, then?"

"That's the solution to the problem."

"Still, I don't think you took drugs just because you didn't have either women or money. After all, you started very young, when you were sure women and money would both be coming your way . . . I wish I knew how it all started. It seems to me that the solution to your problem lies in its beginning."

Dubourg mused and began to doubt. He was not deceived by the incredible pettiness of the dilemma which was choking Alain's life; the very absurdity of this dilemma convinced him that it was only an excuse. And drugs were only another excuse for this first one. Or did when it all started not matter in the slightest?

He despised that childish method of joining physical tendencies and ideas in a cause-and-effect relationship. Physiology and psychology have the same mysterious root: ideas are as necessary as passions, and passions as the movements of the blood. So what could be the use of asking whether it was drugs that produced the philosophy or the philosophy that led to drugs? Had there not always been men who denied life? Was this a weakness or a strength? Perhaps there was a great deal of life in Alain's rejection of life? For him it was a means of denying and condemning not life itself, but the aspects that he hated. Why should he not yield to his impulses and break, without a thought for the consequences, with everything he disliked and despised? Taste is a passion, and worth as much as any other. Why should he settle for women who were neither very beautiful nor very good? Why should he have to work, to perform that tedious and for the most part unnecessary labor which fills our cities with its futile commotion?

But to take that path was to fall back into the mystical protest, into the adoration of death. Addicts are the mystics of a materialist age who, no longer having the strength to animate objects, to sublimate them into symbols, undertake a converse labor of reduction —eroding them, wearing them down until the kernel of nothingness within each appears. Addicts offer sacrifices to a symbolism of shadows to combat a fetishism of the sun—they loathe the sun because it hurts their tired eyes.

No, Dubourg was all for that difficult and modest effort, the human enterprise which seeks not the equilibrium between corporal and spiritual entities, between dream and action, but the point of fusion that annihilates these futile distinctions which are so easily perverted. If he studied the ancient gods, it was not out of a defeated bookishness or a desire to hide in the past, but because he hoped this study would nourish his researches into the inflections of the present. Meanwhile, Alain was dreaming aloud.

"Drugs were in my veins before I knew it."

"What?"

"I started by drinking while I was waiting for women, waiting for money. And now all of a sudden I realize I've spent my life waiting, and I've drugged myself to death."

"But still, you've had Dorothy and Lydia, and others before them."

"It was too late, and besides I didn't have them, and I don't have them now."

"Yes you do—you still have Dorothy. You don't have to sleep with her for that."

"I don't have her, and the reason is that I was bad in bed with her."

"She's afraid of the drugs, that's all."

"But I take drugs because I'm a lousy lay."

Dubourg was alarmed by so many admissions from Alain, who ordinarily avoided such confidences, especially in the last few years.

But at the same time, he couldn't help finishing the analysis he had begun.

"A funny way to live, our lives depending on women," he murmured.

Alain frowned. He saw that Dubourg was playing the cynic to involve him in the kind of confession that leads to remorse.

"I don't see how your life depends on Fanny," he interrupted.

"I've buried myself in her warmth like a hog in his wallow. As for you, you need women even more because . . . You're still a child: women are your only link with society, with nature even."

"Yes, you told me that before, pimps are only old babies. But you won't make me say I'm a pimp. You've always had a pedant's preference for dirty words."

Alain was growing furious; at last he saw Dubourg's bigotry breaking through: he wanted Alain to define himself, and to reform by doing so.

And Dubourg plodded on.

"Look, Alain, I know you think I'm a clod, but you shouldn't mind profiting from my cloddishness. I'm trying to get you to admit you're immoral, which is quite different from pretending to be an immoralist. What makes problems for you now is that you have prejudices you sometimes laugh at yourself."

"Wrong. I never laugh at prejudices, precisely because I have them all. Don't get me started on that."

Alain stood up and began pacing back and forth.

Now Dubourg was furious, and resentful at being so. Yet on this point, he stood fast: one of the surest reasons for Alain's collapse was his refusal to admit he was a lazy man who lived off women. Alain really was the disaffected bourgeois he had denounced a moment ago, a man who saw the vices sprouting from his prejudices, but who was incapable, because of his prejudices, of enjoying his vices.

But he hesitated to go on: he lacked confidence in his abilities. What he was saying explained Alain, but nothing more. Something more intuitive was needed: to love Alain enough to be able to re-create him in his own heart. Alain had been there an hour and nothing had happened. He would leave, dissatisfied with himself and so even more dissatisfied with life, more isolated, more warped. That must not happen!

"Alain, tell me who you are. *Make* me understand you! Let me know you!"

"So you can change me?"

"If you'd shout who you are at the top of your lungs, it seems to me you'd stop being it right away.

Between you and another you, there's only a single step."

"Or a stumble."

Alain stopped pacing and stared with sad contempt at Dubourg, Dubourg who was kind and stupid.

"Listen, you big dope," he said softly, "you know very well who I am."

Dubourg sat with his mouth open.

"Yes."

"And you like me the way I am, and no other way."

"But what good would my friendship be to you unless you felt I wanted to change you?"

A phrase came to Alain's lips; he held it back a moment, then let go.

"I'd like you to help me die."

"Oh, no! Alain, I love life, I love life. What I love in you is your *life*. How can you . . . ?"

"Yes, you're right . . . Oh, if only I could have put myself in your hands!"

"Right!"

"I can't though. You know that."

"You can't?"

Dubourg was humiliated. He knew that to save

Alain, he would have to dedicate himself, give him several months of his life, forget the gods of Egypt for a while, and be inspired by them in reality.

A moment later, he took refuge in anger. What weakness! How little virility Alain had! He had reached the point of expecting charity from others. If he had been a man, he might have asked for Dubourg's support; but not hung on him.

"Alain, I work, I'm patient, and so I get something out of myself. Come and live here with me and you'll see what patience is. You'll start by loving the part of life that's in you . . ."

6 A FEW MOMENTS LATER, ALAIN AND DU-
bourg were walking side by side between the Seine
and the Tuileries. They were sad and bitter.

Dubourg saw that the chance to save Alain had
passed. He was thinking that if he had been really
sure of himself, he would have attacked Alain, in-
sulted him, shouted at him: "You're mediocre, accept
your mediocrity. Stay at the level where nature put
you. You're a man; by the fact of your mere humanity,
you're still invaluable for other people."

But he was not strong enough to treat someone like
Alain that way. And besides, was Alain mediocre,
since he was irreplaceable, inimitable? Wasn't it actually his duty to praise him? In this lost man there was

a secret desire to excel in some part of life, a desire which approval might revive . . .

Yet Dubourg was forced to acknowledge that he could not go far in this direction. He could scarcely admire Alain, much less approve of him. And so he reverted to his first regret. Not being able to admire Alain, he would have to make Alain admire him: and for that he needed to be a more powerful man. In Alain's downfall he recognized his own defeat.

As for Alain, he knew that he was seeing Dubourg for the last time. Dubourg's attitude, among other excuses, gave him every reason for dying: life in his case had not managed to justify itself. It had shown a face disturbed, taxed with misrepresentations, tormented by impotent allegations.

The two friends were walking along the Seine. The river flowed gray, under a gray sky, between gray buildings. Nature that day could be no help to men; the square stones softened in the humid air. Dubourg shivered; the man walking beside him had no recourse: neither woman nor man, neither mistress nor friend, and heaven was silent. Perhaps it was his own fault; since Alain had never learned to count on himself, the universe, centerless, revealed no consistency.

A woman passed them, pretty and elegant. She glanced at them briefly; Alain obviously attracted her. Dubourg smiled and shook Alain's arm.

"You see, you want to touch her. Paris is like that woman; so is life. One smile, and the gray sky clears. This winter we'll go to Egypt together."

Alain shook his head.

"You remember . . ." Dubourg began.

Alain stopped and stamped his foot.

"You're driveling."

They had frolicked for ten years on the banks of this river: all their youth, for Alain all his life.

"I don't want to grow old."

"You regret your youth as if you had *done* something with it," Dubourg blurted out.

"It was a promise. I lived on a lie. And I was the liar."

Saying this, Alain looked at the Chamber of Deputies. What was this cardboard façade, with its foolish little flag? And in front of it, this tide of wheels?

"Where are they going? It's stupid," he snarled.

"But they're not going anywhere, they're just going.

I love what exists—its intensity touches me. It's eternity."

Alain looked at Dubourg one last time. There was something positive in that face. Unbelievable. He had another impulse.

"Dubourg, let's go out together tonight. We'll telephone a friend of Lydia's. She's quite beautiful."

Dubourg looked at him, and laughed quietly.

"No, tonight I'll write two or three pages about my Egyptians, and I'll make love to Fanny. I sink into her silence as if it were a well, and at the bottom of that well there's an enormous sun that warms the earth."

"You're turning into an animal."

"I'm happy."

They were in the middle of the Place de la Concorde.

"Where are you going?" Dubourg asked.

"I have to drop in at Falet's show. Come with me, it's on the rue Saint-Florentin."

The Place de la Concorde was already caught in winter's petrification; dead asphalt swept by dust.

On the rue de Rivoli, lights were coming on.

Alain thought about all his winters. They were the

uncontested triumph of artifice: closed rooms, bright lights, exasperation. The last winter. This last spatter of light on his face. What was Dubourg's life like? A dim, slow death. Dubourg had never left Paris, that lingering, low fever. New York, at least, was an open atrocity. Dorothy was there, between the paws of the monster that writhed and howled and shed torrents of blood from a thousand open wounds.

A narrow street, near the Madeleine. A tiny shop, dilated by raw light. Dubourg entered reluctantly, for he knew Falet.

Falet was in the shop: he was a barely noticeable runt. Across a matchstick spine hooked the circumflex accent of his shoulders. And higher, a patch of gray skin, false teeth, the eyes of a sardine. This foetus had emerged dead from its mother's womb, but had been recalled to life by the sting of a serpent which had left him its venom. In his youth, when his door had always been open, Dubourg had welcomed Falet, who by way of thanks had pierced each of their minds with his little forked tongue.

Dubourg nodded vaguely, turned his back and looked at the walls. Everything Falet did was business, but this particular business was only a pretense. Like the beggar in the street, all his gestures were aimed at the passer-by, to attract and to dupe him, but all to win two sous worth of attention, to keep from vanishing into nothingness.

Subtle people praised Falet because they could classify him: he was a photographer.

In the art of photography, truth is achieved only by deceit; but these deceits are delicate, they correct and annihilate each other to isolate an indestructible residue. Yet Falet the photographer could not dispel the frenzy of Falet the calumniator. He made monsters of all his models; he deformed them, following a sardonic stereotype, and coaxed an emphatic, improbable ugliness out of their faces and bodies. Eventually, beneath fingers stiffened by a desperate malice, nothing of reality remained.

But those socialites who gorged on gossip and diversion until they had become demi-intellectuals, and those intellectuals whose mindless routine had turned them into socialites—in short, all the scum of Paris declared itself enchanted by this new excess, this new impotence.

Dubourg glanced at this museum of horrors with tranquillity. He remembered with astonishment the time when such trivia still bothered him: he was used to vermin, he no longer scratched. But he was even less indulgent of the glibness of phonies like Falet, who disguised beneath a clever coat of varnish—elegance and restraint—his subversive efforts. Efforts which prompted the ladies flitting here and there to exclaim: "Stunning! Stunning!"

Dubourg shook Alain's hand and left.

7 ONCE AGAIN, ALAIN WAS ALONE. THE BAR-
rier that Dubourg raised between him and death, a
barrier of words, vanished like a music-hall act, the
scenery with the clown.

Falet had watched him enter with a sudden qualm,
which was more than confirmed when he realized
Alain was staying. The farce of the cure was over.
Once already, Alain had disappeared, then returned.
Now he was coming back for good.

Alain did not look at Falet, but paced up and down
in front of the photos. He raked up a compliment,
then glanced at Falet who was staring at him.

"Are you still out there?"

"No, I'm not still out there."

"Oh I see . . . You're looking very well. My compliments!"

"You don't look any more like a corpse than usual."

"You pick your friends; you stick to normal types, you're back with Dubourg. That idiot, that bore Dubourg."

Just then a woman came in. A wandering statue. Released from the hands of a Pygmalion (who was only a copyist), she had the ostentatious beauty of replicas. Her shoulders, her breasts, her hips betrayed the faint excess, the redundancy of sculpture of a decadent period.

Eva Canning, born in the Orient, had been raised in London. Nothing was more likely to demoralize Alain than this huge statue: he saw too much resemblance between its illusory power, the air it displaced, and his own sense of the emptiness of things.

This apparition quickened his day. This woman who was laden with a thousand privileges—beauty, health, riches—looked at little Falet with a humble, pleading expression.

"We're going to my place, Eva and I. Are you coming?" Falet asked calmly.

"Yes."

They got into Eva's car, a powerful, silent, indifferent machine.

During the short ride, while the other two chattered on, Alain thought of nothing, or rather thought of everything, but all his thoughts were swept up in a devouring whirlwind in which he heard the rising speed of his fall.

Up a steep staircase somewhere in Montmartre, they climbed to Falet's apartment, an icy, empty studio. In one corner, a camera and a klieg light; in another, a few torn books. A door led to an alcove filled by a rickety divan.

"It's cold," Eva said.

"My darling, the stove you gave me is being fixed."

That meant Falet needed money: Eva looked crestfallen.

"I'll get the blanket from the car," Alain said.

"Nice of you."

When Alain came back with the heavy, fragrant robe over his shoulder, the other two had already settled themselves on the divan, on either side of the opium tray.

"I can't smoke with clothes on," Eva declared.

She got up and slid her dress over her head. Then she pulled off her slip, her garter belt, her stockings. She was completely naked, a magnificent, bloodless plaster body.

Alain emitted a long sardonic laugh. Never had he had so exact a sense of his own impotence. For him, the world was peopled only with empty forms. It was enough to make you scream, it was enough to make you die.

Little Falet, preparing a pipe, tried to catch Alain's eye. Eva, who had no more belief in other people's desires than in her own, wrapped herself in the blanket without even looking at Alain; he turned to Falet.

The little creature's expectant grin suddenly relaxed; he pointed to a cupboard.

Drugs were everything, there was no use trying to get away from them, the world was drugs.

Alain opened the cupboard and took out a vial. Then he removed from his pocket the syringe he had

brought from Doctor de la Barbinais's. He filled it
with heroin, rolled up his sleeve, and stuck the needle
into his arm.

He kept his back to them for a moment, staring at
the wall. Then he was done, it wasn't difficult. Acts
are fast, life is over quickly; soon comes the time of
consequences, the time of the irreparable.

Already his immediate past seemed incredible. Had
he really dreamed of curing himself? Had he really
shut himself up in those abominable sanitariums? Had
he sent Dorothy a telegram? Had he held Lydia in his
arms?

He turned around to take a good look at Eva
Canning: beauty, life were made of plaster. Everything was simple; everything was finished. Or rather,
there had been no beginning, there would be no end.
There was only this moment, eternity. There was
nothing else, absolutely nothing else. There was nothingness.

Eva sucked on the pipe Falet had prepared for her;
then she rolled over in the blanket, exhaling a little
smoke. One of her hard, polished shoulders shone gold
in the light from the little lamp. This fragment of a

broken statue rolled across a desert, lay in
of a warm and soothing abyss.

The waves multiplied and broke one ov
Alain was not returning to drugs; he had never left
them. That's all it was, but it was that. It was of absolutely no interest, but neither was life. Drugs were
only life, but they were life. Intensity destroying itself
proves that everything is the same as everything else.
There is no intelligence because there is nothing to
understand, there is only certainty.

*Suicide? Why bother, life and death are the same
thing. From the point of view of eternity where I am
now, where I've always been, where I'll always be.*

*The proof that life and death are the same thing is
that I'm walking up and down in this room and that
I'm going to telephone Praline, because I go on as if
nothing had happened, while in fact nothing has happened.*

"I'm going to make a phone call."

"I don't have a telephone. Try the bar at the
corner."

"All right."

He had already felt like leaving, like going somewhere else. The night was beginning. Night, perpetual motion. One had to keep moving, going from one place to another, never staying in one place. To escape. Escape. Intoxication is movement. And yet one stays in the same place.

"You're not very polite, leaving already."

"My dear Falet, I'll be back right away—I'm going to make a phone call."

He stood for a second in front of Eva. She was no longer plaster; though she seemed immobile, she was in the throes of movement.

"Good-by." And she burst out laughing.

"Good-by."

Alain went down the stairs.

You wonder why they make stairs. Where they lead. Nothing leads anywhere, everything leads to everything. Rome is the starting point of all the roads that lead to Rome.

Someone was on the stairs ahead of him.

Huge crowds go up and down stairs.

"Excuse me."

"Go ahead, go ahead, I can't walk fast."

It was a heavy man with a gray mustache and a

pipe. Alain remembered the face; he was a sculptor quite well known to the discerning; not too famous, not too rich, unpretentious. He probably lived in this building. He looked shrewd, kind, clever; he smelled of tobacco and benevolence.

But despite his slow movements, he too was swept along by the furious torrent of life, by drugs. Alain stopped on a step and looked back at the old man.

"If I closed my eyes, your statues would turn to dust and you'd be out of luck!"

The old man stopped too, a flash of amusement glowed in his clear eyes, then he went on.

Alain felt like crying, waved, turned on his heel, and went down the stairs four at a time.

Outside, he hailed a taxi.

8 ALAIN JUMPED OUT OF THE TAXI AND
entered a bar on the Champs-Elysées. He would
telephone from here: it was much pleasanter than a
bar in Montmartre. He enjoyed public comfort, and
returned to his rut with a grim voluptuousness. For
years, evening after evening, he had telephoned like
this from bars to certain apartments, from these apartments to bars.

He felt the panic rising. When vitality diminishes,
its vestiges are revealed by its haste to consume itself.
Alain ordered a whisky, went into the telephone
booth, told Praline he was coming, came out, went
over to his glass on the bar.

Then he glanced around him a little; faces had not
changed in ten years. In a corner stood three or four

cramped-looking gentlemen with insipid eyes who
had been young before him. One had run to fat, another had lost his hair; but they displayed the same
dim smile.

They knew Alain and disapproved of him.

"Did you see that face? Drugs."

"He married a woman without a sou."

"He's through. He used to be something, though.
Richard was wildly in love with him. If he had
wanted . . ."

Alain drank his whisky. The stares no longer had
any effect on him: he wasn't interested in pleasing
now, men or women; he was through pleasing.

It was here that he had taken heroin for the first
time, in the lavatories to the right. They hadn't been
made of marble then. He had been with Margaret at
the time. Another American. She was young, pretty,
elegant; her smile gave the illusion of a lacerated
tenderness. She used to tell him that she would never
forget him.

Those gentlemen there at the end of the bar disliked
him for not joining their camp; but a few experiments
had made him feel a revulsion he could not overcome,

despite his approval of experimentation. Yet he liked their company, for with them, he was free to dream about women.

He had stood in bars, as at this moment, for hours, for years, all his youth. People looked at him, he looked at the others. He waited.

He finished his drink. He paid. He left. Outside was the Champs-Elysées, puddles of light, infinite mirrors. Cars, women, fortunes. He had nothing, he had everything. Whisky and drugs chased each other, galloping in waves, burning and cold, but regular. Habit. Beneath it all, an inexorable rhythm.

Abstract stages: having taken another taxi, he stared into space, looking neither right nor left. Out of the city that rose and fell on either side emerged only fleeting images, a few personal memories. Alain had never looked at the sky or the housefronts or the pavements—palpitating things; he had never looked at a river or a forest; he lived in the empty rooms of this morality: "The world is imperfect, the world is bad. I disapprove, I condemn, I annihilate the world."

His family thought he had subversive ideas. But he had no ideas, he had an atrocious lack of them: his mind was a pathetic carcass picked clean by the vultures that hover over the great empty cities. He got out of the taxi and paid the driver munificently. A thousand-franc note, one small flame among others in this total conflagration. He had to burn these ten thousand francs in a few hours. For this fetishist, such little acts assumed enormous importance and absorbed all reality in their childish symbolism: throwing away a thousand francs equaled dying. The prodigal's hallucination is as great as the miser's.

He rang at Praline's door.

9

"I'M LEAVING MY OLD FRIEND DOCTOR DE la Barbinais," Alain said, sprawling in a huge armchair opposite Praline's divan.

No one said anything, at first; but the same certainty showed on three faces.

Praline raged to herself: "Why this pretense of a cure? He's never stopped, at this very moment he's full of heroin."

Finally, she snapped: "What are you going to do?"

She made no effort to conceal her irony, nor did she repress a glance, which Alain could not help noticing, toward Urcel, whose annoyance she knew was as intense as hers.

Alain replied with a sardonic laugh. Since these

three addicts were so sure he shared their fate, there was no use talking; that way, at least, they would be deprived of an admission they were only too eager to hear.

Praline, who had just finished a pipe, moved away from the tray she shared with Urcel and as she thrust her short squat body down into the cushions, she stared at the quiet fire burning in the little stucco fireplace.

The walls were bare, the scant furnishings consisted of a few rudimentary lines. It might have been a storeroom full of packing cases. Several low lamps. When she received uninitiated guests, Praline hid the pipes and trays in a chest on which they sat, vaguely alarmed, vaguely attracted by the odor that hung in the air. The initiated watched them out of the corners of their eyes and waited for them to leave.

"I'm not asking personal questions," Praline began again, "but what now? Will you stay in Paris? Will you go back to New York?"

"I have to go back to New York."

"Need money, Alain?"

When Praline became nasty, she tried, by making

her voice more caressing, to deceive herself about it.

"Sure."

Praline shrugged. Another of Alain's annoying characteristics. Why hadn't he promptly and openly per-
formed the actions which would have assured him his
share of the things of this world? Resourceful herself,
she liked resourceful people. Drugs didn't keep her
from looking out for her own interests. Indeed, more
than one deal had been made in the glow of that little
lamp, there, on her left.

To show her impatience, she changed the subject
abruptly.

"Would you like something? . . ."

She stopped a second. Was she going to add:
"Would you like to smoke with us? Would you like
some heroin?" No, since he was keeping quiet, they
would treat him like a hypocrite. Having paused no-
ticeably, she continued: "I mean: Whisky? Champagne, perhaps?"

"Champagne! I remember a young lady I used to
drink champagne with . . ."

Alain blushed; he had not meant to answer in kind.
He had long ago given up attempts at repartee, for

which he was not gifted; if he had occasionally passed for a dangerous conversationalist, it was because of his blunders. An allusion to the old Praline stirred the air of this close room too vigorously. Opium dens are places where it is unbecoming to refer to the past. Praline had once been as fresh as childhood. In her eyes, all images were gay; the blood ran bright and full in her lips. Men came to her in crowds, but none had stayed.

"Of course, I'm no longer a young lady, but I can still offer you champagne . . . since you've been weaned from other things."

"No, whisky."

Praline rang. An old butler came in, and soon brought Alain what he had asked for. This man, whose hair and teeth had been wrenched out by smallpox, moved about without looking at anything around him. Why should he? He knew what had to be said to the police. Moreover, he toned down his reports, for he needed Praline and her influential friends to protect him against his immediate superiors, who were tired of the troubles his nocturnal obscenities caused.

Alain poured himself a glass of whisky. There was a rather long silence.

Urcel, who had arrived shortly before Alain, was gorging himself on his first pipes, which kept him from talking as much as usual. But his bulging pupils, as he stared at Alain, leaped from his thin face under the receding forehead, while from time to time his skinny legs stirred in his empty trousers.

Alain avoided looking toward the darkest corner of the divan, where, like a poor relation at the end of the table, Totote, the horrible Totote, had her lonely opium tray behind Urcel's back.

From time to time, a soft crackling was audible; then an odor of tropical cooking filled the room.

After a long puff, Urcel finally spoke. He regretted breaking the silence which he had enjoyed as an evidence of Alain's hypocrisy, but the desire to speak was always so strong for him that he sometimes seemed carried away by a generous abandon.

"The cure . . . funny business, eh?"

"Funny business."

There was another silence. Then they heard Totote's sharp voice: "The gentlemen are so formal."

Alain had tried to give Urcel his opening, but he was afraid the sobriety of his answer had discouraged him. So he dropped one or two remarks.

"The cure. You'd like me to tell you about it. What for? You know as much about it as I do. I remember how you suffered, last year."

"And now you. Poor Alain."

That mealymouthed tone of addicts, and underneath the nastiness of old cats.

Totote again: "It's touching."

Urcel had made a long, painful, completely ineffectual attempt at a cure, and it had taken him a long time to admit his defeat. Alain's eyes, bright with the agonized pleasure of his relapse, exasperated him. "I'm no stronger than Alain," he was forced to say.

He had to prove the contrary immediately; he had to show Alain the difference between them, make him feel his power. But to defend himself, or to launch an attack, he had never imagined any better tactics than to be ingratiating. He needed to wallow with his adversary in a subtle degradation. His meager vitality

could show itself only in the reactions of his epi-
dermis; Urcel's life was a perpetual mimicry.

He began his ruse of the day—he would adorn himself with sentiments that ought to be dear to Alain.
But first, he had to exorcise by words a certain intimate demon that ceaselessly tormented him.

"Why pretend to cure oneself, my God! Out of kindness, to please a few worried friends, so as not to leave
humanity alone in its unhappiness. But we didn't wait
for drugs to bring us to the limits of life and death."

That *we*, which forced complicity and simulated
equality, infuriated Alain. He compressed his lips and
replied: "One tries to cure oneself to keep from dying,
because one's afraid of being dropped by this bitch of
a life."

"Yes indeed, one's afraid," Totote giggled in her
corner.

Urcel shied at Alain's determined tone; yet he went
on—by standing pat, not advancing toward his goal.

"Once cured, we'd find ourselves exactly where we
were before the cure—hopeless."

Alain assumed a bantering tone: "Despair is one
thing, drugs are another. Despair is an idea, drugs are

a practice. A practice that scares us so much that we hope against hope to cure ourselves."

Urcel, in his turn, found the *we* unpleasant.

"No, that's not it," he answered, his tone half-offended, half-joking. "It was an illusion, a leftover from the horrible intoxication of life."

Alain saw Urcel's strategy: to escape regrets, to keep from admitting defeat, he was inverting the situation and denying that he had made an effort. How could you lie to yourself? Yet most of them, their minds fogged, easily managed to deceive themselves. But a mind like Urcel's? He got drunk on words and, to be able to go on talking, never stayed alone.

Alain, who wanted to see all that weakness come to something, held his peace and merely voiced a rather general reflection.

"Let's not pretend to be subtler than we are. There's absolutely no way of being subtle in this world. Even the most delicate soul can only walk on its own two feet."

Immediately Totote cried: "It's own two feet! I like that. It's own two feet, there you are."

She twisted her miserable body on the cushions.

Praline followed the game with sharp eyes. She snapped at Totote: "Shut up, no one's listening to you. Smoke."

Urcel, who had started now, seemed impervious to mockery and made his circular gesture.

"We could have done something besides take drugs, but we'd have always needed something that satisfied our craving for risk."

Alain, apparently noticing nothing, mused aloud: "There are a few other vices besides drugs, but none as decisive."

Urcel thought he had been approved; he repeated complacently: "None. Since we had risk in our blood . . ."

That was the way, he thought, to please Alain—by talking about risk. And to please him was to dominate him, since it was to deceive him. All life, for Urcel, lay in that sequence: he could only deceive because he was never himself, but to deceive people gave him the sense of possessing them.

Yet Alain broke out laughing in his face.

"Risk! There are drugs and drugs. Your opium's an easy way out."

"With or without drugs, anyone who has a genuine sensibility stands on the brink of death and madness."

"You won't die."

"You don't think so?"

Alain suppressed a too insolent smile. When Urcel felt someone was about to see through him, impudence became audacity.

"I've always felt I was in this world *and* in another," he blurted out.

"No! In another! How can you be in two places at once?"

"Hasn't it ever happened to you?"

Alain looked disgusted.

"I used to believe that, when I could still get drunk on words, but it was all a horrible joke. Nothing moves."

"That's what you think!" Urcel exclaimed indignantly.

"It is."

Urcel was trying to rescue the poetic prestige of drugs.

"Still, there's a kind of warping. Everything . . ." he began.

Alain cut him short.

"Drugs are life, even so; they're stupid, just like life."

"Oh, no! They're life, but touched by a certain ray of light. It's a state of awareness that's quite salutary. One knows both sides of the question; one has a foot in each world."

"Oh yes, I forgot, you believe in the other world."

Alain had stopped laughing. He picked up his glass of whisky and took a long drink. He was not proud of despising so much a man whose cunning he had once mistaken for delicacy.

Urcel made a face, he felt that he had gone too far. He had been calling himself a Christian for the past few months, but he prided himself on not angering the libertines among whom he had always lived. His skill had deteriorated; in Alain's presence he ought to have said the same things without religious overtones. Beneath Alain's easy realism, which offended him as anti-poetic, he feared a moral stringency. But he had to go on.

"My dear, you're not going to quibble with me over words," he cried, raising his voice. "I never play with words, I use the ones that are useful to me. I realized one day that the words I was using were those of the mystics: was that any reason to deprive myself of them? Now look, you're not a fanatic, you loathe systems, you'll admit a fact which is foreign to none of us: all of us, in one way or another, have the feeling that we can't put the best of ourselves, our brightest spark, into our everyday life, but that at the same time it's not wholly lost. Don't you feel that way? The impulse that wells up in us and that seems stifled by life isn't lost; it accumulates somewhere. It forms an indestructible reserve which won't vanish the day our flesh fails, and which guarantees us a mysterious life . . ."

Urcel stopped. Totote released a rasp of anger. Alain watched Urcel with growing malice.

"I've never felt anything in me but *me*."

But just as a longer protest boiled up in him, he stopped short. He was astonished at the new development Urcel's cunning had suggested: one that could dupe only the person who used it. In the very act of self-deception, Urcel insured his own tranquillity. First he told himself: "I'm not lost because I smoke, I smoke because I'm lost"—a reasoning Alain knew well. Then he added: "Anyway, my loss is only an appearance; what I lose on one side I gain back on the other."

Alain was incapable of worrying about what might be more serious in such reasoning than Urcel's fraudulence. He had no idea of what it is to be a Christian: he could not imagine that need to revive, with all the windows closed, what one cannot stand in the open air—that paradoxical taste for life which, having denied it in one realm, reproduces it in another.

But in the present case, it took only a little good taste to be scandalized by the ease with which a dabbler in feelings and ideas took possession of an attitude the moment demanded.

Then too, Alain, especially when other people were concerned, never despised the facts. He was not forgetting that Urcel desperately pursued young men. What afforded him an initial success harmed him later on: he surprised them, but soon wearied them with his inexhaustible chatter. The result of these disappointments was that Urcel felt chilled: he sought the warmth of Praline's lamp. Formerly, one took to drink.

Those were the facts: but hypocrisy played its part, prompted by fear.

Alain compared Urcel to Dubourg, who was also beginning to transpose his vitality, in order to save what was left of it in a world that could not be verified.

Perhaps this operation is common to all men who live on imagination and thought, especially when they reach middle age. But Alain's passion, his madness, though he had never lived at all, was to suppose one can live in a single realm, on a single plane, that one can engage all one's thought in each of one's gestures. Unable to do so, Alain wanted to die.

Yet incapable of arguing, he repressed as well as he could the interjections that filled his throat; he merely repeated in a low, furious tone: "I only know *me*. Life is *me*. After that, there's death. I may be nothing, but death is nothing twice over."

Urcel abhorred violence; fearing Alain's anger, he stifled his resentment of the other's blind hostility. Behind those curt words, moreover, he still sensed that rigor which impressed him. Yet he had to speak: first, to dispel a terrifying silence, and second, to protect his own skin, by defending these ideas that suited his vices and weaknesses so well. So he continued with an almost suppliant gentleness: "What we call life and what we call death are only certain aspects, among others, of something greater and more secret. We die as fast as we can to attain something else . . ."

Totote reared up among her cushions like a serpent that has been attacked.

"Why are you afraid of words? Go ahead and say the one you keep rolling over in your mouth: God."

Urcel kept his back to the poor woman; but he shrugged his shoulders with horror and glanced reproachfully at Praline.

Praline looked at Totote with amused contempt. Why did she let this poisonous toad in? Thanks to her small fortune, Totote had managed to hold on to a man who had once been Praline's lover and who had left her. And now Praline kept this hideous lump of flesh within reach, exacting a slow and intermittent revenge.

The man was dead. Weak and stubborn, credulous and eager to brag of his own importance, he had jum-

bled together several ideas which he imagined consti-
tuted an act of total subversion. Obsessed with the
idea of God, he called himself an atheist, but all his
frenzy had ended in Manicheism: he saw double, and
spoke incessantly of a God and a Devil who were al-
ternately identified and opposed. He imagined himself
a communist, but his thought was so shallow that he
was content with a revolution that would culminate in
catastrophe and had never given a thought to what
must follow. He was also a sadist. Finally, he had
killed himself on drugs. Totote had inherited his hates.

She flung herself into the silence they left around
her.

"You know, I ought to bless you, Urcel, you're the
best blasphemer I've ever known. No one can make a
better hash of religion than you. It does my heart
good to hear you mixing up drugs and prayers like
that . . ."

"That's enough," Praline cut in.

After a pause, Urcel said to Alain: "But to continue:
nothing will stop me from believing that we can
understand one another. Your love of risk . . ."

His timorous nature betrayed him: he had felt the need to turn to Alain for support against Totote's attack. But then he had forgotten the precaution necessary in dealing with Alain. He had just repeated a word which, from the first, had awakened Alain's mistrust.

"Risk! So you think you're running a risk? What risk?"

Urcel tried to hide his mounting fear behind a smile of astonishment.

Alain's voice had trembled. Regaining control of himself after a moment, he continued: "You've found a nice little system to keep you happy. Anyway, what risk are you running? You smoke? Some smokers live to be seventy. The only risk you take is the risk of stupefying yourself!"

Alain stopped, looked at Urcel, and suddenly broke out laughing. He realized that the conversation had finally come full circle: half an hour's chatter had brought them to this notion of risk by which that old hypocrite Urcel had hoped to ensnare Alain.

Leaning back on the cushions, Urcel raised a tortured face to heaven.

"Of course, in the long run, if you live less, what you write loses by it," Alain concluded slowly. "And then what happens? But maybe the idea bothers you? Maybe the idea bothers you very much? Maybe that would be the sort of risk you keep mumbling about."

Alain had gone too far. Suddenly Praline hissed at him: "It's easy for you to talk."

Alain shuddered.

"It seems to me you once thought of writing. Have you forgotten the satisfactions you probably expected from it?"

Alain was immediately silenced. And yet, when he denied Urcel the right to mention risk, he did so because risk was obviously something more serious to him than it was to Urcel. He himself had taken the first path he had come to, but he was determined to follow it to the end: nothing in the world could have stopped him now.

But Praline had just struck him at a sensitive spot. More than once he had wondered: Doesn't all my disgust come from my mediocrity? Still, he remembered the brief return to paper and ink he had made the evening before; he could tell himself he would have had to be possessed by an urgency much stronger than Urcel's to consider prolonging his desires and his life by writing.

Besides, he knew the old rancor that fed Praline's severity. He had met her when she was still trying to live. In those days people drank champagne at her place, no one smoked, and at daybreak she would ask one of the men who was still there to stay. But two hours later he would make his escape disappointed, for she had nothing left to give, having squandered it all in the night's coquetries.

Yet Praline, reading Alain's thoughts, wanted to challenge him.

"Urcel runs a greater risk than anyone else, because he has more to lose than anyone else."

Alain shook his head, his face inscrutable.

"He must complete his work," she proclaimed.

In her excitement, she forgot her habitual restraint and became emphatic.

Urcel seemed upset.

"Please, my dear . . ."

"His work—what's that?" Alain growled.

"When you have something inside you, it has to come out. You don't know anything about it."

"When you have something to say, say it once—you don't have to repeat it."

"My poor friend, you have no sense of such things."

Alain, paler than ever, took a drink of whisky. He suddenly stared at Urcel.

"You've been writing a hell of a long time."

Praline was about to intervene again, but Urcel silenced her with a gesture.

Alain sprawled back in his armchair, savoring a certainty that was no less acceptable for being bitter. Again he compared Urcel to Dubourg and decided: "That's what ties them to life: their work!" He became even more attached to his idea of gratuitousness. Naïve dandy that he was, he assumed everything could be swift, ephemeral, immediate—a brilliant trajectory that disappears into nothingness.

Despite Urcel's warning, Praline spoke her mind again.

"You make me laugh. You'll choose the same way we did, between drugs and life."

Alain slowly lowered his eyes.

"That's enough," Urcel cried, annoyed by Praline's awkward assist.

Praline suddenly seemed ashamed. Instinctively, she knew Urcel; she knew that like herself, he was brutally egotistic and without any real feeling for others. Yet she admired him for occasionally adopting all the appearances of feeling in, as she thought, so successful a manner. She felt incapable of such skill herself, and suffered a certain humiliation because of it.

But on the other hand, she had learned from life never to let people get used to stepping on your toes.

"You know, it might be better for you not to come here any more, and not to smoke any more either," she shot at her old friend.

Immediately she was afraid, not of having offended Urcel, but of the prospect her words afforded. "Opium's robbing me of the last years of my youth, if it's robbing him of his talent."

Still, with her old vitality, she could not take such a dismal view for long. She quickly corrected herself.

"I'm joking, Urcel, you're like a salamander. Alain,

ask him to show you his new poems, they're exquisite."

"And that settles everything," grunted Totote.

For a moment, Urcel had been feverishly preparing
a pipe.

Alain got up and began to pace back and forth.

"What a disgusting performance," he groaned to
himself. "How humiliating life is. But death will see
me before these others."

There was, after all, something of the Christian in
Alain. But beyond the Christian, there was a man
who, if he accepted his weakness as a matter of
course, still resisted coming to terms with it, or trying
to turn it into a kind of strength; he preferred to steel
himself against it until he broke.

"I'm leaving."

He got up and went over to Praline to say good-by.
This abrupt movement changed the atmosphere.
"Now where is he going?" they wondered.

"My dear Alain, you'll come back to see us soon?"
Praline asked anxiously.

"We need company," Totote whined.

"Of course I will."

"I'm very fond of you, we're old friends. You mustn't be sad."

"Urcel will read you his poems," Totote added.

"Good-by, Alain," Urcel said, blending all his feelings in a smile: coquetry and fear, hate and love.

"He's become impossible," Praline cried once he had left, "actually he's nothing but a has-been and envious to boot."

"Don't talk nonsense," Urcel snapped, "he's a very nice boy, and a very unhappy one."

"Yes, that's right, he's very unhappy," Praline concluded. "It will all end badly . . . but he won't kill himself."

"How do you know?" wheezed Totote.

They went back to their pipes.

10

WHY DID ALAIN GO ON? HADN'T HE
seen enough? If he wanted to kill himself, what better
time than seven or eight o'clock in the evening, when
all desires, released from captivity, rush in a whirlwind
at top speed across the city? But life is only habit, and
habit holds you as long as life holds you. As on all the
other days of his life, Alain continued on his nightly
rounds, which started at five in the afternoon. Now it
was time to visit the Lavaux'.

Terrible to go to the Lavaux', always terrible, more
terrible than ever. The house, to begin with, was too
pleasant. Lavaux's mother, who despite her fortune
had known how to enjoy life in a free and noble
manner, had had the idea of building a beautiful stone
house with doors and windows—nothing else. No or-

naments, only essentials. But the essential is the most perfect ornament.

It was all simple and solid, and made Alain realize each time he came that there was something his character or his environment had deprived him of forever: the ability to accept life firmly and frankly.

In front of this façade, Alain stopped a moment. He was not drunk, he had had only three whiskies. He had no particular desire for another injection: the mere presence of the drug, even a minute dose, sufficed. He congratulated himself on being dressed properly for the Lavaux', where he was always awed by the prevailing harmony.

He went into the salon; through the group which pressed around her, he reached Solange Lavaux.

She held out her hand to Alain with that smile of gratitude she gave all men, for all men desired and cherished her. In that generation, there would not be another beauty so perfect, and so at ease in her perfection. Parvenus had not yet taught this princess arrogance.

A warm voice rang out. Tall Cyrille Lavaux, so thin,

so straight, held out his hand to Alain. His ugliness
was as seductive as his wife's beauty. The love he
surrounded her with was so healthy, so simple, so gay
that she seemed a more perfect creature because of it.

Lavaux slowly took Alain around to greet his other
friends. There were three men and three women.
Alain knew all the women and two of the men.

"You know Marc Brancion?"

"No."

"Well, that's one way of putting it."

It *was* a way of putting it, in fact: everyone knows
heroes. In the old days you saw them in the forum,
now you see and hear them in the cinemas. And soon,
by television, their most intimate retreats will have
glass walls; then a total fraternity will prevail.

Brancion had the face of a hero: a complexion made
livid by fever, teeth broken in some brutal accident.
One stared with respect at this man who had stolen
and killed, for he had done so of his own volition,
unlike most of the heroes of our time.

Alain looked at Brancion, who did not return his
look.

"Would you like some port?"

Lavaux, who always had excellent port, refused to serve cocktails. He kept up his mother's tradition. And his father's . . . Perhaps, but he had several fathers to choose from: a prince, a painter, an actor from a working-class family. Sensibly enough, he stuck by his mother, and enjoyed the rich mystery, the rare freedom, of being a bastard.

"Dinner is served."

They walked from the salon into the dining-room. The appealing thing about the house was that it was not empty. Not too many things, but each one in exquisite taste: furniture, paintings, objects. Whatever seemed unnecessary had its secret use. It was different from Praline's.

Good food, prepared by a country cook, well simmered and redolent of the open air.

Alain sat down and looked at them all. These beings from whom he was forever separated pleased him.

Except Mignac, who was too much like himself, or at least had been too much like himself. He hated Mignac.

Alain found himself sitting between Anne and
Maria. They were Brancion's former wives; his present wife, Barbara, was on Cyrille's right. Brancion
was on Solange's right, beyond Anne. Every time he
returned to France, he had to marry within twenty-
four hours a woman whom he would abandon for
good the day of his next departure.

"He's had women, he's stolen and killed, he knows
Asia like the palm of his hand. He'd dislike me if he
knew me; but he won't know me; he'll never even look
at me.

"All these people are alive; you could even say
they're beautiful. Mignac's cheeks are ruddy with
health. He got to bed at four in the morning, rode for
two hours before noon, then went to the Bourse,
where he made money. Yet I used to make the nightly
rounds with him, and he was as incapable as I of taking hold of life.

"What are they talking about?"

It seemed that one talked about nothing when sitting next to Anne. Was she stupid? A pointless question. She was peaceful, she laughed happily, she had a

lover who satisfied her. She had deceived him at first, but gradually she had been absorbed by him, and now she slept, snug in the heat of her master's entrails.

Cyrille talked loudly, laughed loudly, conversed with everyone at once. This hour was his reason for being. He was devouring, with neither unseemly haste nor deliberation, the tenuous fortune his mother had left him; he had already sold the house in Touraine. From one end of the year to the other, he and his friends celebrated Solange, her abundant and delicate body, the utterly terrestrial enchantment of her smile.

She had a succinct morality: pleasure. But her pleasure was easily identified with that of others. At sixteen she had left her family, which was rich but dull, and had become a courtesan. A real courtesan, capable of joy, a Manon. Now she was married to Cyrille, to whom she had given daughters as beautiful as their mother. She had already been married twice before, the only signs of weakness that could make this courtesan liable to comparison with a woman of the world. She needed money, but no more than Cyrille. Money to inspire love, love to inspire money. For the moment, she loved Cyrille. She always loved for a long moment. As Rimbaud might have said, "O seasons! O beds!"

Did she like Brancion? Brancion was better than Cyrille, better than Mignac, better than Fauchard, better than everyone.

"Brancion, my friend Alain's staring at you," Cyrille shouted.

Brancion looked at Cyrille, not at Alain, laughed coldly and went on talking to Solange. Cyrille was not jealous; he counted on keeping his wife for several years, he made love well, he still had two million francs ahead of him. Afterward? But afterward his youth would be over. Besides, he would be quite capable of reforming completely.

"The confidence, the tranquillity of these people," Alain kept thinking, gaping like a child who is given the crudest, the simplest ideas by grown-ups and forgets to take advantage of them.

What good is such ingenuousness?

At Solange's left sat Fauchard, who had taken Maria after Brancion. Maria was Russian. A Russian peasant with a face and a body carved out of wood. Although he was atrociously bald, one-eyed, badly

dressed, clumsy with words, she loved Fauchard. She
had refused to marry him, but she lived in his house.
She slept, played with his dogs and his children, lit
cigarettes, ate candy. She never opened a book and
could barely write the five or six languages she spoke.

Fauchard, the son of a self-made man, had hesitated
before deciding to replace his father at the head of
his factories, for he preferred spending his time in sec-
retive love affairs, and needed only a little money. Yet
modest as he was, he was not exceptional enough to
reject a task he regarded his responsibility. Thereafter, he had stifled his immoderate inclinations without complaint, and proved punctual, capable of reflection and decision. But on the other hand, he rejoiced
that a woman like Maria should so easily adopt the
liberty he had refused for himself; he was one of those
men whose heart, disciplined and enlarged by work,
can transpose its own pleasures to another. In this
man, despite his somewhat morose aspect, there was a
hidden elegance that charmed Alain. But Fauchard
paid no more attention to Alain than Brancion. Alain
would have liked to please them all, except Mignac.

"In this house, I'm in exactly the place I'd have

liked to live, where I ought to have triumphed. I'd like Fauchard to like me."

But he also wanted Brancion to like him; and the women. The latter, moreover, did find him attractive; each of them threw him a friendly, rather vague smile over the shoulder of the man she was with. The Lavaux liked him too.

"I'm liked by everyone—and no one. I'm alone, quite alone. After dinner, I'll leave."

Cyrille watched him out of the corner of his eye; he felt that vague solicitude which Alain aroused in everyone and which mortified him so much. But with Cyrille, this impulse took the form of trumpeted sallies.

As he finished a long swallow of Montbazillac—he had recently received a barrel and was delighted to be able to offer his friends its warm delicacy that evening —he shouted: "Every time I see Alain, I remember this magnificent scene: at seven in the morning, a policeman finds a young man stretched out on the tomb of the Unknown Soldier, dead drunk and sound asleep. The said young man was so sure he was home in bed that he had put his watch, his wallet, and his change beside the flame as if it were the lamp on his bed-table."

Brancion turned away from Solange and asked curtly:

"What? . . . Who's the hero of that story?"

Cyrille released a huge burst of laughter.

"Alain here. It's the best joke I know."

Brancion turned toward Alain, calmly watched him go pale, then turned back to Solange.

The sweat stood out on Alain's forehead. Worst of all, Solange's eyes met his. Submissive to Brancion's authority, she mocked him without dislike, without pity.

There was a silence, and every face tensed. But Cyrille, with a flood of gestures and words, already freed himself and the others of all shame.

From the other side of the table, Alain endured Fauchard's pitying gaze; Mignac had the tact to refuse to look at him.

It was over.

He drank. Anne and Maria turned kindly to him, but suddenly he was drunk. Drunk with shame.

"I'd have liked to be like Brancion," he whispered to

himself. "Since in any case, whoever you are, you want the same things as everybody else, you have to go out and take them away from others. Then you can despise everything, everybody. But not before. Before, you're a cripple who spits on people who walk straight. I've dishonored my fine feelings of contempt. My life should be stamped out."

They left the table. As they passed into the next room, he groaned again in a low voice: "I'm an idiot."

Some stayed in the dining-room, others went into the salon, the library, Solange's boudoir.

Cyrille took Brancion by the arm and explained who Alain was. In Paris, Brancion looked at everything from a great distance, as though he were still in Asia, except for what concerned his immediate interests, to which he devoted the greatest possible care. For the person Cyrille was defending, he showed the same disdainful indulgence he granted Cyrille.

"If you make me talk to him, I'll hurt him even more," he said calmly.

"Sometime during the evening, you could find a moment to say a kind word to him."

"I doubt it."

Brancion smiled. He wore his dentures with osten-
tation; women were not put off by them.

Cyrille ran back to Alain in a corner of the library.

"I'm sorry I caused that misunderstanding between
you and Brancion. I know you like him, and if you'd
met him in Asia, he'd have liked you."

"Poor Cyrille, you're wonderful. Nothing that con-
cerns me has any importance. I haven't gone to Asia.
It's atrocious not to exist and still walk around on two
feet, because then your feet hurt terribly. You don't
know how much my feet hurt."

Cyrille couldn't help looking at Alain's feet, then his
eyes flicked back to his face, where alcohol struggled
with panic. He held a glass of brandy in a trembling
hand.

"But I'd be happy," he continued, "to congratulate
M. Marc Brancion on the services he's rendered in
Asia to the cause of . . . Ah! Here he is!"

Brancion was crossing the room to rejoin Solange
and his wife in the boudoir; he stopped abruptly.

"I want to tell you, monsieur," Alain began in a
tone he meant to be firm, but which sounded bom-

bastic, "I want to tell you that I find it no funnier than you do to go to sleep on a tomb, when it's so much easier to open it and go to sleep inside. Doubtless the poor man would have made room for me . . ."

He had started a long speech, but unable to get rid of the solemn tone which clung to his words, he stopped short, hoping to redeem himself by being concise.

"That's all," he broke off.

"I beg your pardon," Brancion replied as though he had not heard a word, "but I never get drunk, and I dislike stories about drunkards. Besides, I didn't quite catch the story Cyrille was telling."

"You prefer hashish to alcohol," Cyrille remarked acidly.

"I've taken hashish, as well as other things," Brancion snapped.

"I'm only a drug addict," Alain tried again. "Drugs are stupid. Addicts and drunkards are poor relations. In any case, we disappear fast enough. We do what we can to oblige."

Alain stopped again; he was pleased, he had added

the grotesque to the ignominious. Brancion, hands in his pockets, was staring at a painting over Cyrille's shoulder; Cyrille was on tenterhooks.

"Alain," Cyrille said, completely at a loss, "you are pretty far gone."

"No, I'm not far gone, but I'm going—it's late."

"Don't do that, please stay."

"I'll stay, but I'll be gone soon."

He turned to Brancion.

"You know, I'm a man; and I've never been able to get hold of money, or women. And yet I'm energetic and quite virile. But there you are, I can't reach out my hand, I can't touch things. Besides, when I do touch them, I don't feel a thing."

He held out a trembling hand and looked at Brancion, begging for a moment's attention. But Brancion had listened to humanity once and for all, had closed his ears to this concert of beggars, sidewalk charlatans, and sentimental pickpockets.

Cyrille was still racking his brains to establish a contact between the two men when Solange came looking for him.

"Say hello to the Filolies, they've just arrived."

Alain felt another tug at his heart: Carmen de Filolie, the most beautiful, the richest woman in Chile. Another chance he had missed.

He tried to connect with Brancion once again.

"I admire your actions because you don't believe in them."

"You're mistaken, I believe in them with all my heart; but I beg your pardon, I must go say good evening to Madame de Filolie."

Alain found himself alone in the library. He wanted to run away, to regain the night, the street, but as he put his hand on the knob of a door that led to the staircase, Fauchard came in, with Mignac at his side.

He stepped back, seeing Alain alone, but Alain, without looking at Mignac, rushed toward him.

"Do you believe in your actions too?"

"My dear fellow, insofar as I know you, if I say yes, you'll despise me, and if I say no, you'll mistrust me."

"You don't believe in your money, but you believe in Maria, is that it?"

"I don't much like to talk about myself."

"Then you don't like to talk at all."

"I like to listen a great deal."

"Businessmen, sitting in their armchairs, sometimes listen to lazy people talk or even sing. I'm lazy, but I can't talk any more, I'll never talk again."

"What's the matter with you?" Mignac asked with a concerned expression.

He remembered the years of fear and loneliness when he was poor, when he had looked for miracles in the arms of a pretty woman.

"Fauchard, I congratulate you on having found Maria," Alain continued.

Fauchard's face lit up in spite of himself: he frowned at the same time that his mouth smiled.

"Anyway, you have a wife, I have nothing. You don't know what it's like not being able to put your hand on anything."

"Really," Mignac said.

"We have anything we want, but we have nothing *unless* we want it. And I can't want, I can't even desire. For example all the women here—I can't desire them, they frighten me. I'm afraid of women the way I was afraid of the front, during the war. Take Solange —if I was alone with her for five minutes, I'd turn into a rat, I'd disappear into the wall."

"We'll see about that," said Mignac.

He went out and came back with Solange, then took Fauchard away.

A much more beautiful woman than Dorothy, than Lydia, and much more amorous.

"What's the matter, Alain dear? You're a little drunk, and so sad. What is it now? After all, you've gotten over drugs. And the beautiful Lydia? And the beautiful Dorothy? And the beautiful who else?"

"They're gone. They're not beautiful enough, not good enough."

"They're ravishing, they adore you. Which do you prefer? Are you keeping them both?"

The kindness of women where he was concerned! He enjoyed a certain prestige in their eyes, but what was its nature? He had moved some of them quite deeply, but they easily resigned themselves to giving him up, leaving or never even launching an affair.

"I'm finished, I can't even move my little finger any more."

He stretched out a drunken little finger.

"You're getting maudlin now."

"Oh, I'm not drunk, I can't get drunk. I couldn't lose

my head any more, except on the guillotine. I'd go look for it around the Place de la Concorde, but I wouldn't find it."

He stopped, and made an enormous effort to control himself, to concentrate on what he had to say to Solange.

"Listen, Solange, you understand, you *are* life. All right, listen, life, I can't touch you. It's awful. You're there in front of me, and there's no way, there's just no way. So I'm going to try death, I think that will work. It's funny, life, isn't it? You're a beautiful woman, you like to make love, and yet between the two of us, nothing doing. Isn't that funny?"

"It's a question of the moment, Alain, between a man and a woman."

"Women are always *taken*."

"No they're not, Alain. I know a lot who are waiting for you."

"They're waiting for me so hard they forget all about me."

"No, they're looking for you."

"They're not looking, they're waiting."

"Perhaps they want love as much as I do—the real thing."

"Ah, you see, *the real thing.*"

He was speaking louder and louder, his voice jerky, his face convulsive.

Cyrille came to the door; Solange sent him away with a gesture.

"I never learned how to take care of myself, but all the same, just once, someone ought to have taken care of me."

That was what he had never dared say to men. A supplication—at least it would have been better than nothing. There can be great strength in real supplication.

"To leave without ever having touched anything. I don't say beauty, kindness . . . with all their words . . . but something human . . . and then you . . . you can do miracles . . . Touch the leper."

"Alain."

Solange's heart was full of the silly, flighty vanity of a kitten, but she had also a genuine feeling for life, a healthy warmth. She realized how serious the moment was; she knew men, knew when they were suicidal or when they were merely joking, she had seen so many of them collapse at her feet or in her bed. Perhaps she would have to sleep with this one; that would give him back his heart.

Cyrille and Brancion came in. And it was all up with Alain; Solange glanced at her husband's lithe figure, at Brancion's battered face.

"I'm leaving," cried Alain, "I have to go somewhere."

"No, stay, you have to talk some more," Cyrille said, with the semblance of authority his nervousness gave him.

But something of Brancion's will power had passed into Alain. He made an effort to calm himself, to throw them off the track.

"Someone's waiting for me."

Brancion looked at him, for a second.

"I'll come back, but I have to go now."

"Then you'll come to lunch tomorrow?"

"Yes, of course."

"Oh no," he told himself, "tomorrow I won't be hungry."

He went as far as the door of the library. He saw all those men and all those women, sitting or standing, chattering majestically, amid the sweet odor of good cigars.

"I'll find a way to avoid them forever."

He turned to Cyrille, who asked him: "Do you want to go out the other way?"

"Yes."

"Enough humiliation," he thought.

He kissed Solange's hand; she could not detach herself from Brancion, and said to him distractedly: "See you tomorrow, Alain."

Cyrille went down with him to the great tiled vestibule.

"I hate seeing you leave like this. What's the matter? Why didn't you spend the summer with us?"

Cyrille was very nice, but he hadn't sent a single telegram, hadn't tried once to save him. Like Dubourg.

"Are you in trouble again? What the devil, if you can't do without drugs, take some. Smoke a little, that will calm you."

"I hate opium, it's a drug for concierges."

"Get married."

"I'm vowed to celibacy."

"Do you need money?"

"I have thousands of francs in my pocket."

"Come to lunch tomorrow, we'll spend the day together."

A long and happy day with a charming friend, in a perfectly appointed house. Day in, day out. No, the street, the night.

"Good-by, Cyrille."

"Good-by, Alain . . . Alain, wait. Alain, you do like us . . ."

"Yes."

The street.

11

He always came to his senses in the street; and even on the stairs. Once away from people, he found his tongue.

The November night was beautiful: cold made the city brittle and empty; still, out of habit, he looked for a taxi. He hurried along with a gait that for a man of thirty was heavy and jerky.

It seemed to him that the evening was drawing to a close, yet it was only eleven. That used to be just a beginning, and tonight he wondered how to kill another three or four hours.

Finally, he found a taxi; he sank into it, and gave the address of a bar at the foot of Montmartre. He was following his old rounds, step by step. In those days, after the cinema, he would spend an hour there before going to the nightclubs.

The world was filled with people he would never know. He would kill himself tomorrow, but he had to get through the night first. A night is a winding road that must be followed from one end to the other.

At this hour, all women belong to men: Dorothy is in the arms of a strong man with muscles of steel, with fistfuls of banknotes in his pockets. Lydia is in the arms of gigolos, each handsomer than the one before, so that she is obliged to leave one for the next. Solange will soon go to bed in Cyrille's arms, dreaming of Marc Brancion.

Women and men clutch each other. What brutes men are! They're all alike—devoted, but not to life: to their tasks. And what tasks! Egyptology, religion, literature. Then there are the men of money: Brancion, Fauchard. Those are the real men.

"Their world's closed to me, closed for good. And that's where the women are.

"There's nothing to be said against the world of men and women, it's a world of brutes. And if I kill myself, it's because I'm not a successful brute. But the rest—

thought, literature—oh! I'm also killing myself because I've been wounded there by an abominable lie.
Lie, lie. They know there's no such thing as sincerity,
yet they go on talking about it. They talk about it, the
bastards. But I know I'm not lying to myself. If I die,
it's because I have no money.

"Drugs? No. Look: I only took one shot tonight. So?
I'm only drunk on alcohol, and besides, I'm not even
drunk. Of course, I'm going to have another shot, this
heroin's got to be good for something. Here's the bar,
I'll go to the toilet . . ."

And thus Alain was driven into the cell, he who had
revolted against Urcel and his pseudo-mysticism. The
necessary conclusion of a morality of disgust and
scorn.

But Alain, in that place, did not confine himself to
meditation, nor did he dream. He was taking action,
injecting himself, killing himself. Destruction is the
opposite of faith in life; if a man, after eighteen, man-
ages to kill himself, it is because he is endowed with a
certain sense of action.

Suicide is the resource of men whose springs have
been devoured by rust, the springs of the quotidian.

They were born for action, but they put it off; and then action comes to them on the pendulum's return. Suicide is an act, an act of those who are unable to perform any other.

It is an act of faith, like all acts. Faith in a fellow creature, in the existence of others, in the reality of relations between the self and other selves.

"I'm killing myself because you didn't love me, because I didn't love you. I'm killing myself because we were always apart, to bring us closer together. I'll leave an indelible stain on you. I know very well that one lives better dead than alive in the memory of friends. You never thought of me, all right, you'll never forget me!"

He raised his arm and stuck in the needle.

This bar was rather elegant and filled with brilliant waifs and strays: men and women devoured by boredom, corroded by nothingness.

Alain was sorry about Solange. Until that evening, he had never thought of making love to her, paralyzed by the thought of Cyrille's mastery. And suddenly this woman, so easy, so difficult, represented for him all he was losing. He felt a terrible regret for the flesh, so real now. Human beings walked and sang in a paradise, life; the procession advanced, led by Solange and Brancion. Even Dubourg walked at the end. He thought again about Dubourg, about the gray Seine— he would never see the Seine again. But why not, he was in no hurry, he still had money, drugs. No, without Solange, impossible to survive.

He left the bar, hailed a taxi, and drove to another bar two hundred yards away. The heroin was rising in him again, but as though after a tidal wave, the water entering through a breach and lapping what no longer defends itself.

"There's a friend. Standing in front of the bar, like me, alone. *Mon semblable, mon frère.* He'll listen to me."

Milou was a good fellow whose scruples, by restricting his weakness, accentuated it: he did not always take the money he was offered, and thereby convinced himself of his own honesty, a deplorable illusion which hid his worst weaknesses from himself. He had neither trade nor family, only a few stray friends here and there. He was good-looking, and that had to compensate for his failings, but now he was getting old.

With tacit accord, Alain and Milou left the bar to walk in the street. Milou had been struck by Alain's expression.

"You look as if you'd seen something extraordinary."

Milou knew Alain took drugs, but he could tell that something else was the matter.

"No, nothing . . . I saw Dubourg, Urcel, I had dinner at the Lavaux'. Oh yes, it's true, I've looked at people the way I've never looked at them before."

"Yes, that happens sometimes . . ."

"Sometimes, yes."

They were walking toward the Opera, through the empty streets.

"You know, it's too bad I have no charm," Alain continued.

"No charm, you!" Milou protested with an energy that revealed his candid admiration. Alain revolved in a circle above his own; while Milou only approached people in bars, Alain followed them into their salons.

Alain shrugged his shoulders slowly.

"No, I don't have any charm. Some people find me pleasant enough, and then, others . . ."

"Call it what you want, people like you."

"No, they don't. No one's ever liked me. At eighteen, when I was quite handsome, my first mistress made a fool of me."

"That's to be expected. Everyone's a cuckold at eighteen."

"But it hasn't stopped since. Always very nice, but they go away . . . or they let me go. And men . . ."

"Don't you have friends?"

"Friends are like women, they become indifferent."

"It's hard to believe what you're saying."

"It's exactly the way I'm telling you. I'm awkward, I'm heavy-handed. I've tried like hell to make myself lighter. Inside, I'm delicate enough, but my hands are clumsy."

"You pretend to be awkward to be funny, but you do it on purpose."

"That's what fools you. I knew I was awkward, so I tried to be funny. But I've never been able to accept a clown's success and nothing more."

"But you're only like that at odd moments."

"That's all my life is—odd moments."

"But what would you like to have done?"

"I'd like to have captivated people, kept them, attached them to myself. So that nothing around me would ever move again. But everything has always slipped away."

"So what? Do you like people all that much?"

"I'd like to have been loved so much I'd think I was the one who was doing the loving."

"I know what you mean, I'm like that. But, just between us, I don't know if that's enough."

"I've always been as grateful for kindness as anyone else: I'm not a hog."

"Yes, gratitude's something. But you know, from there to love is still a long way . . . And besides, even when we really have love in our hearts, will that hold people?"

"You're only loved as much as you love. It sounds stupid to say that, but it's true."

"No, it's because we're too grateful that people don't give a damn about us."

"We're grateful, but we don't want to take them. That's it, you have to make people feel you want to take them, and when you've taken them, that you can keep them."

Alain stopped. He looked straight ahead of him at the rue Scribe, a street like any other. He took a bitter pleasure in summing up his life. Milou looked at him and grew afraid. They lit fresh cigarettes and walked toward the Madeleine.

"You're right, Milou, I've never loved people, I've never been able to love them except at a distance. That's why I've always left them, or made them leave me—to have the necessary perspective."

"No, I've seen you with women, and with your best friends: you fuss over them, you never let them alone."

"I try to put them off the track, but it never works . . . Yes, you see you must never lie to yourself—I regret terribly being alone, not having anybody. But I only have what I deserve. I can't touch, I can't take, and basically, that's what I'm really like."

"Maybe you're right. But you mustn't say things like that. Thinking like that turns a man into a rabbit. It makes you want to . . ."

He stopped in horror, not daring to look at Alain.

"When you really care for people," continued Alain,

who had noticed Milou's silence and savored he fleeting premonition, "they're nice to you, they give you
everything: love, money."

"Do you think so?" Milou asked with childish greed.

Alain turned off the rue Royale and reached the
Champs-Elysées by the rue Boissy-d'Anglas. At the
corner of the avenue Gabriel, they ran into a prosti-
tute.

"Good evening, mademoiselle."

She was well known to regulars on this beat: Alain
had accepted her services once or twice, but she
couldn't recognize him, for thousands of men had
passed through her hands.

"Good evening, gentlemen," she rumbled in an old
drunkard's voice. "Looking for a bit of fun?"

"No," said Alain, "we're having fun by ourselves."

"You could take me along too. I'm game for anything."

"For nothing."

"I like to please."

"Well, good night."

"Good night, darling. A cigarette?"

She was decked out in a second-hand motley whose colors had blended and faded in the rain. She gave off an odor of dirt and alcohol as she extended a gnarled hand toward Alain's pack of cigarettes. Her face was an old, capsized sun.

"If you see M. Baudelaire, tell him good night."

"M. Baudelaire! Who do you think I am?"

They walked on.

"What was I saying?" Alain asked.

"That people would give you everything if you loved them."

"Yes, but I wonder if you *can* love them, after all. They love lies too much. Everyone, everyone I've seen today. They're all alike, it's a joke: Urcel's as grotesque as Dubourg."

"No, Urcel isn't fooled by big words like Dubourg."

"Don't be silly! Urcel's an author, an author's always taken in by words. If there's one thing people are taken in by, it's their profession."

"Even us?"

"Of course, us too. Doing nothing's a profession, after all, everybody knows that."

"So what are we taken in by?"

"We think that if we do nothing, it's because we're more sensitive."

"Oh! I don't think so, I'm lazy, that's all. I'm not ashamed of being lazy, but I don't brag about it either."

"But deep down inside you, you think that you're sensitive. I think so, I can't *not* think so. I'd have liked people to like me, but I lack a certain knack. And actually, that knack disgusts me."

"So what should we do?"

"That's just it."

"Do you still take drugs?"

"Do you still drink?"

"I can't any more, I can't even lift a glass. As far as love is concerned, that's still easy—I have a talent for it."

"Not me."

"Not you! Funny, I'd have thought so."

"I'd have thought so too."

"It's the drugs that get in your way."

"You know, explaining . . ."

They walked along the Champs-Elysées a long

while without speaking. Milou was sleepy, but he didn't dare leave Alain.

Alain walked without looking at anything, as he had always done . . . And yet the avenue was beautiful, like a broad shining river that rolls in majestic peace between the feet of the elephant god. But his eyes were fixed on the little world he had left forever. His thoughts wandered from Dubourg to Urcel, from Praline to Solange, and farther, as far as Dorothy, Lydia . . . For him, the world was a handful of human beings. He had never thought there could be anything more to it. He had never felt involved with anything larger than himself. He knew nothing of plants, of the stars: he knew only a few faces, and he was dying, far from those faces.

They walked slowly back up the Champs-Elysées; they were both tired. Alain was prolonging this last human contact, letting the empty taxis go by. Any one of them might have taken him back to the sanitarium. Milou was afraid to be left alone with the thoughts Alain had given him. The cafés were closing; they sat for a moment on a bench, without speaking.

All of a sudden, Alain said in a dead voice: "So,

everything will work itself out. A year from now we'll be rich and happy."

He glanced out of the corner of his eye at Milou, who immediately reached out for this note of reassurance.

"You really think so?"

"Are you sleepy?"

"Yes."

"Well, good night then."

Alain jumped up, shook Milou's hand without looking at him, and hailed a last taxi.

12

WAKING. THE LEAD WHICH, AT THREE in the morning, has sealed his eyelids and his limbs dissolves in heavy layers. But all at once a notion of deliverance stirs and works in his body: *now I have entered the zone of death.*

There's time anyway. But he looks at the crumpled banknotes on his table; he feels no desire to spend the rest of them. As for the syringe, there, on the night-table, it is used up, used up. At last he can stay in bed. But Alain has never loved his bed. Not sensual enough. No temperament.

He rings for tea, and speaks kindly to the slovenly chambermaid who is not at all pretty. He tells her he won't be getting up until lunch: it is eleven o'clock.

Little by little he awakens, he shakes off the night's

vapors, he gets up. What a face! Everything is carefully arranged, in the bathroom as well as in the bedroom.

He sits down, pisses, shits. He wipes himself, gets up, reties his pajamas. He looks at himself in the mirror. What a face! The look of his worst days is already smeared over his features. He brushes his teeth. He lights a cigarette, he reflects. He has a lot of things to do this morning, before lunch: telephone Cyrille to tell him he won't come to lunch or to tell him he will come; telephone Dubourg. Why? To tell him to come see him this afternoon. No, don't telephone Dubourg. No mail. Nothing from Dorothy. No cable from Lydia. Ah! The prickly circle of loneliness contracts around him. He'll have to kill himself. Yet there's still all that money to get rid of, there on the table. After all, he spent very little yesterday. A few more days, but what's there to do? Where can he go? Whom can he see? Well, there are drugs. That's worn out—too slow, not enough. Take an enormous dose: he's done that several times; he practically blew himself up. He didn't die, but he could die from it. To kill himself that way, what cowardice!

No. Then?

There's the revolver, over there, between two shirts, in the closet. Yes, but he mustn't touch it until he's absolutely sure. There's still time because the decision is already taken. Meanwhile, there's the money. But this absence of women, this silence of women is permanent. The impossibility of seeing friends again. Listening to them repeat themselves.

"I'm going to get dressed. But then, lunch with Mademoiselle Farnoux and Madame de la Barbinais, the *table d'hôte*, the everlasting *table d'hôte*.

"I can stay in my room, have lunch in bed.

"I'm going to lie down again, I'll read. There's that detective story . . . It's quite possible to lose myself for two or three hours in a detective story.

"Why not?"

. . . .

"A telephone call for you."

How long had Alain been reading?

He put on his bathrobe and slippers and went downstairs.

"Hello!"

"Is that you, Alain?"

"Oh, Solange!"

"Yes, it's me, Alain, how are you this morning? Cyrille's gone out. I'm calling to remind you that we're expecting you for lunch. Don't come too late, you and I can talk. Are you all right?"

"Not bad, not bad."

"*Not bad.* You say that so oddly. But you will come, won't you?"

"Of course, of course I will. It's kind of you."

"I'm very fond of you."

"You're very fond of me. And Brancion?"

"Oh! Brancion's different, he's the opposite of you, he's a force of nature."

"Do you like forces of nature?"

"I love them, I love everything."

"I'm not a force of nature."

"You have a heart."

"I don't understand a word. Good-by, Solange . . . Hello . . . You think I have a heart?"

"Of course."

"Seriously?"

Alain went back up to his room four steps at a time.

"Solange doesn't want anything to do with me. Solange doesn't love me. Solange has just answered me for Dorothy. It's all over.

"Life wasn't going fast enough for me, I'll speed it up. The graph was sagging, I'll send it up. I'm a man. I'm the master of my flesh, I'll prove it."

Propped up comfortably, neck on a pile of pillows, feet braced at the end of the bed, legs apart. Chest out, naked, well exposed. You know where the heart is.

A revolver is solid, it's made of steel. It's an object. To touch an object at last.

A NOTE ON THE TYPE

THE TEXT of this book is set in *Caledonia,* a typeface designed by W(ILLIAM) A(DDISON) DWIGGINS for the Mergenthaler Linotype Company in 1939. Dwiggins chose to call his new typeface Caledonia, the Roman name for Scotland, because it was inspired by the Scotch types cast about 1833 by Alexander Wilson & Son, Glasgow type founders. However, there is a calligraphic quality about this face that is totally lacking in the Wilson types. Dwiggins referred to an even earlier typeface for this "liveliness of action"—one cut around 1790 by William Martin for the printer William Bulmer. Caledonia has more weight than the Martin letters, and the bottom finishing strokes (serifs) of the letters are cut straight across, without brackets, to make sharp angles with the upright stems, thus giving a "modern face" appearance.

W. A. Dwiggins (1880–1956) was born in Martinsville, Ohio, and studied art in Chicago. In 1904 he moved to Hingham, Massachusetts, where he built a solid reputation as a designer of advertisements and as a calligrapher. He began an association with the Mergenthaler Linotype Company in 1929, and over the next twenty-seven years designed a number of book types for that firm. Of especial interest are the Metro series, Electra, Caledonia, Eldorado, and Falcon. In 1930, Dwiggins first became interested in marionettes, and through the years made many important contributions to the art of puppetry and the design of marionettes.

Composed, printed, and bound by
The Haddon Craftsmen, Inc., Scranton, Pa.
Typography and binding design by
HERBERT H. JOHNSON

A NOTE ABOUT THE AUTHOR

PIERRE DRIEU LA ROCHELLE was born in Paris in 1893. At the conclusion of World War I (during which he twice was wounded in combat), he became a regular contributor of poetry and fiction to the *Nouvelle Revue Française*, and frequented a coterie of friends—Aragon, Éluard, Breton—who were to form the nucleus of the Surrealist group. The late twenties and early thirties were his most productive period as a novelist. Though he continued to write fiction thereafter, his work revealed an increasing preoccupation with politics and with his visionary conception of a united European state. During the Occupation, he accepted the directorship of the Vichy-sponsored *Nouvelle Revue Française*, though he frequently used its pages to prophesy the doom of the Nazi cause. An enigma to friends and enemies alike—and perhaps to himself —he committed suicide in 1945.